JOYCE SWEENEY

FREE FALL

LAUREL-LEAF BOOKS

Published by
Bantam Doubleday Dell Books for Young Readers
a division of
Bantam Doubleday Dell Publishing Group, Inc.
1540 Broadway
New York, New York 10036

Lines from "The Enemy," "De profundis clamavi," "Autumn Song," "Spleen," and "The Little Old Women," all by Charles Baudelaire, are taken from the 1986 Penguin Classics Edition, translated by Joanna Richardson. Penguin Books, Ltd., London. Acknowledge Curtis Brown on behalf of Joanna Richardson. Copyright © Joanna Richardson, 1975.

ISBN: 0-440-21975-2

RL: 5.1

Reprinted by arrangement with Delacorte Press

Printed in the United States of America

October 1997

10 9 8 7 6 5 4

Randy was circling the perimeter of The Chamber, like a dog marking territory. "This has to be the same place my cousins were talking about."

Terry took off his pack and sat on the ground. "So, good. I feel so much better. Now let's call them and ask them how they got out of here." He turned his round face up to the ceiling and the sunbeam illuminated him like a picture in a religious magazine. *The choirboy at prayer,* Neil thought. Then there was some very subtle change in Terry's expression. A narrowing of the eyes, a tightening of the jaw. Suddenly his mouth opened wide. "HEEEEEEEEEEEEEEELP!" he screamed. "SOMEBODY PLEASE HELP US. PLEASE." His voice frayed into hoarseness. "Please. Please." His head lowered. His shoulders rounded and began to shake.

"There might be somebody out there," Terry choked out. "They might hear us. We have to get out of here. I want out!" He covered his face with both hands.

Want OUT.

David put a hand on Terry's shoulder. "It's okay. We all feel like that."

Neil's eye was drawn to Randy, who was moving toward David and Terry with increasing speed. He had a look of purpose about him. Neil had the terrible idea that maybe Randy was planning to slap Terry to his senses, like Patton and the crying soldier.

To my writing teachers: Daniel Keyes, the late Walter Tevis, Jack Matthews, Bill Baker and Gary Pacernick. From all of you I learned not only how to write but how to teach.

ACKNOWLEDGMENTS

I would like to thank Stuart McIver for his invaluable assistance in researching the Florida caves, snakes and sinkholes. Also, thanks to Lee Richardson for setting up the printer and to Dr. William Rea for miscellaneous medical advice.

As always I am grateful to my husband, Jay Sweeney, and my friends Joan Mazza and Heidi Boehringer for helping me "weed and feed" the early drafts, and to my agent, Marcia Amsterdam, and my editor, Michelle Poploff, for assisting me with the final polish.

ONE

9:00 A.M., SATURDAY

Neil saw David lurking in the doorway to their room but refused to look up. He tugged extra hard on his Nike laces to show he was not a man to be messed with today.

"Going someplace?" David asked. Heartbreakingly casual.

"Yeah." Neil finally raised his head. Fifteen-year-old David formed an S-curve against the door jamb. He was a gymnast, made of elastic. His blond hair, catching the morning sun, glinted like water.

"A .date?"

"No."

"Going someplace with Randy?"

Neil decided to stand. He felt inferior sitting on the floor. It was important to tower over David sometimes, to remind him who was older and bigger. "Yeah, with Randy. So?"

"So nothing. I just asked a question." David flopped across the bed and propped his chin on his fists, staring at the privet hedge outside the window as if it were full of interesting sights.

"I suppose you don't have anything to do to-

1

day." Neil felt angry and guilty at the same time. As always. He opened the armoire and fished out a backpack.

"I *suppose* it wouldn't matter if I had anything to do or not," David replied. "And anyway, who said I would even want to go anywhere with you two geeks?"

"I don't know." Neil unzipped the canvas pack and rummaged inside. He found an ancient bottle of Coppertone and a wad of crumpled Kleenex. He dumped the whole mess into the wastebasket. "I just thought today was like every other Saturday where you try to horn in on what we're doing."

David twisted around like a snake, flushing. "What planet are you from? I'd die first. You think I like your foul-mouthed, rude friends? What are you and Randy doing today that's supposed to turn me green with envy? Checking out the Museum of Natural History?"

Neil found an old water pistol in the depths of the backpack, aimed it at his brother and fired. Sadly, it was empty. He wondered what to pack for a trip like this. Not sunglasses . . . "Randy found out where there's a cave. West of here in the Ocala National Forest. So we're going to check it out."

David's blue eyes softened. "A cave? I didn't know there were caves in Florida."

"Well, geeks like Randy know about these things. His cousins explored it and said it was unbelievable— passageways and those crystal things and a pool in it somewhere. . . ."

David sat up and leaned forward, his torso forming

a sharp angle. "Isn't something like that dangerous? Do Mom and Dad know you're doing it?"

Neil found an old canteen and sniffed it. It smelled like a penicillin factory. Did he even need to take water? Was a go-cup too small? A Thermos too big? He and Randy weren't exactly seasoned explorers.

"Hey, did you hear me?" David said. "Did you get permission to do this?"

Neil knew he couldn't show fear. He faked a yawn. "What's dangerous in a cave? Maybe a bat shits in your hair . . ."

David laughed. For just a second he looked like the little kid who used to tag after Neil and hang on his every word. Neil felt royally guilty for leaving him out. "Look, do you want to go with us? Obviously you're going to blackmail me if I don't invite you. . . ."

David went all coy, now that his dreams had obviously come true. "Can I bring a friend, too? I don't want to be like a baby, tagging along with the older guys."

Even though that's what you are. "Not that stupid little Terry Quinn!"

"He isn't stupid. And he's my best friend."

"Anyone who's your best friend is automatically stupid."

"Yeah, yeah. Look, I'm putting up with Randy Isaacson and his rapier wit. You can put up with Terry Quinn, who is very cool and worth enough money to have you bought and shot."

"Maybe so, but the real question is, how am I going to put up with you?"

3

"It's better with four guys, anyway." David slithered under the bed after his sneakers. "It's safer."

"Oh yeah. I'll feel tremendously safe with *you* along." It was supposed to be just more of the same insulting banter, but then Neil realized the words he'd said. "Oh. Hey . . ."

David pulled out from under the bed, rearing like a cobra. "You don't need to say stuff like that!" His blue eyes kindled with rage.

"I didn't mean—"

"When are you going to let up? It's been two years! When is anybody in this family ever going to let up and let me get on with it?"

Neil held out a shaking hand. "No. You—"

"I'm going to go call Terry." David pivoted toward the door and marched out. "Although I don't even know why I want to go now!"

"Wait!" Neil called. Then he hated himself. Now he was begging the kid to tag along and he'd have to spend most of the drive playing up to the little jerk to get him back in a good mood.

And even that would be okay if just once Neil could get to say those things David was so afraid of hearing. That was the trouble. Neil didn't really want to apologize. He wanted David to know that what happened two years ago should never be forgiven. Or forgotten.

―――

Terry's house came first. It was a waterfront property just beyond the Granada bridge, easy to spot because of the two sailboats tied up at the dock. One good thing about David's friendship with Terry, as far as Neil was concerned, was that once in a while, you got a ride on one of the boats. And every Fourth of July, you had the best seat in the house for fireworks, sitting on the Quinns' dock, watching Mr. Quinn barbecue in a canvas L. L. Bean apron. The Quinns were always springing for parties and treats for little Terry because he couldn't get any normal friends by himself.

Except David. David and Terry had been friends since the second grade, the only way to explain such a mismatched pair. David, a golden boy, a lifeguard, captain of the diving team even though he was only in the tenth grade. David, who spent nine tenths of his time on the phone letting girls down easy because they all wanted to go out with him.

Then there was Terry. Running out to the car now with his Mark Cross leather backpack, his yellow polo shirt, shorts too loose for his little hips, brown ponyhair flopping in his eyes. He was fifteen, like David, but he didn't look a day over twelve, with his English-boy complexion and his sweet expression that called out to bullies everywhere, *Please put my head in the toilet. Please snap a towel at my ass.*

Randy Isaacson, never one to mince words, had made up a nickname for Terry the first time he saw him. The Gingerbread Boy. It was perfect. As he jumped into the car now, excited about the upcoming adventure, Terry's eyes were big and round, like brown M&M's. Still, it would be a mistake to take Terence Quinn III for a fool. Hadn't he picked for a best friend the most popular kid in school, who was known for his loyalty and explosive temper? No one had ever picked on the Gingerbread Boy yet and gotten away without a beating from David. David had been expelled three times, all Terry's fault.

The two of them high-fived each other enthusiastically. Quite a coup, getting into the big guys' adventure. "Hi!" Terry said to Neil. "This is immensely cool. You guys are really nice to include me."

"Don't give me any credit," Neil said, pivoting the car inside Terry's circular mosaic driveway. "The kid here was holding his breath for you. Randy is going to shit when he sees I've turned this expedition into a baby-sitting party."

"Expedition!" David shot back. "You and Randy couldn't find your way out of a drugstore! Give me a break!"

"I'd love to give you a break," Neil said, glancing at his brother in the rearview. "You just tell me which limb or digit you can spare."

"Well, it's nice of you to have me, anyway," Terry said. He was like that. Rumor had it his parents screamed at each other day and night and Terry had turned himself into a little diplomatic corps to keep the peace.

Finally they came to Randy's apartment building. Neil felt a rush of joy—someone mature to talk to. Still, he braced himself for attack. Randy wouldn't like seeing the younger guys in the car.

Randy shared a crummy little two-bedroom apartment with his mother and two sisters. His "room" was a sleeping bag on the dining room floor. It was not a good story. Randy's father was an attorney with a fluffy new wife and a big house on John Anderson Boulevard, to which Randy and his sisters were invited about three times a year. Randy suspected a baby was on the way, too, which he felt would make the "old family" really obsolete. Still, Randy and his mother and sisters were a loving, close-knit group, perfectly united in their contempt for Mr. Isaacson. Neil liked to go to Randy's place because it was the only family he'd ever seen, including his own, where everybody seemed to be on the same team. Also, Neil had a head-banging, testicle-throbbing crush on Randy's sister Chloe, but he'd decided to keep that to himself. He didn't know if Randy was okay with interfaith dating and he didn't want to wreck a good friendship.

Randy loped out to the car, swinging his backpack like a weapon. He looked sharp as usual, in black jeans and a black sweatshirt with the sleeves cut out. He had tied a black bandanna around his wrist, probably in the hope that someone somewhere might mistake him for a gang member. Randy was almost as tall as Neil, but where Neil was a muscle-rack, Randy was all sinew. Randy had moved up to Ormond Beach from Miami two years ago to find himself the only Jewish boy at Seabreeze High. Unprepared for such a shock, he at first kept to himself, skulking through the hallways, rushing home to eat lunch. Neil was immediately interested. He'd been born to right wrongs. He invited Randy to come with him to basketball tryouts. When Randy was done laughing, he'd given Neil a quick overview of the historical relationship between Jews and basketball. "So, you'll be different," Neil had said. "You're tall, you're quick and now I know you're overly defensive. To me, that's a born basketball player."

Just to prove Neil wrong, Randy went to tryouts. They both made first string. "Nobody ever proves me wrong," Randy had said. "I guess this means we have to be friends." Now, in their senior year, they were the stars of the varsity team and their friendship was only getting stronger with time.

Randy swung himself into the front passenger seat as if he hadn't seen the younger kids and tossed his backpack over his shoulder, hitting Terry Quinn right in the nose.

"Ow!" Terry said.

Randy swiveled as if surprised. Then he turned to Neil and narrowed his eyes. "Aw, man! What is this about? I said we were going to explore a cave, not take in Disney World!"

Neil started the car up again, twisting to look at the street behind him before shifting into reverse. "Don't make a big thing out of it," he said. He was always cautious of Randy when he was angry. Ever since last year when they lost the championship and Randy went to the showers and pulled five sinks out of the wall.

"Don't make a big thing out of it? This is a whole different deal now! We'll have to be careful of every little thing so they won't get hurt!" Randy ran his hand through his curly hair.

Neil had learned from dealing with David, another hothead, that keeping your voice low diffuses tantrums. Usually. "I was planning on being careful anyway," he said quietly.

Randy bounced in his seat. "Aw, man!"

David leaned forward. "We're not that much younger than you, and we can take care of ourselves."

Randy was glaring out the window now. "Yeah, you probably take care of each other when nobody's looking," he muttered.

"What?" David reared up, jerking on Neil's headrest so he could half stand. "What did you say?" He gave Neil's headrest a shake. "What did he say?"

Neil wasn't feeling optimistic about this day anymore. Keeping one hand on the wheel, he reached back and gently pried his brother's fingers off his headrest. "Nothing. He didn't say anything. Sit in your seat or I'm going to stop the car. In fact, if you all can't get along any better than this, tell me right now and we'll just turn around and go home. I don't need to play referee all day."

"Who asked you to?" Randy said.

"Yeah!" said David. "Who died and made you God?"

Terry Quinn unzipped his backpack. "Would anybody like an oatmeal Scotchie? My mother made them."

For some reason this made everyone laugh. They each took a cookie, and there was a blessed silence while they chewed.

"You better tell me which way I'm going," Neil said to Randy. "I'm not God, you know."

Randy smiled. "Okay. There's two routes we can take but the way I figure it . . ."

Neil settled back in his seat. Harmony was restored, at least for now.

————

The Ocala National Forest, according to Randy's calculations, was an hour's drive from Ormond Beach. They took Route 40 West, almost a straight shoot. On the map, the forest looked like a big green football field. Somewhere off Route 40 was Old King's Road, which was supposed to lead to the cave.

Once the suburbs of Ormond were gone, the landscape was monotonous: corridors of scrub pines lining the road on both sides, nothing to look at but the occasional roadkill or tire casing.

It was late October, finally cool enough to turn off the air-conditioning and roll all the windows down. Neil felt the usual rush of pleasure he got when wind was hitting his face. He would do anything: water-ski, bicycle, ride roller-coasters, anything to get that wonderful wind-in-the-face sensation. It made him feel free. When he was little, his parents were always dragging him in from the yard during thunderstorms. Even though he was terrified of the killer Florida lightning strikes, he'd stay outside to feel that special, green-metallic storm wind in his face. Every wind was different, too, he had learned. If you were free-falling, like from a diving board, the wind was steady and warm and seemed blue. Bicycle wind was silver white. Night wind was purple and very soft and terrifying. The wind inside the car now was breeze, a bouncy light yellow wind that smelled like roots and stems and gave a feeling of promise. Naturally when

Neil was having thoughts like this, he kept them to himself. It was like the secret he had about Baudelaire.

"Can I ask you guys a question?" Terry said. "Did anyone tell their parents what we were doing today?"

There was a brief silence. "We didn't," Neil said.

"I didn't either," Randy said. "My mom's a worrier. It's usually better to just tell her what I've done, instead of what I'm going to do."

"Yeah," Terry said. "That's what I thought, too."

There was another silence. "Yeah," Neil said.

10:00 A.M., SATURDAY

After Barberville, the landscape began to change. Neil didn't like it. He was a child of the seashore, used to flat, clean spaces and big rectangles of blue sky. Now the land had become rolling and the woods were layered up over the hillsides, leaving just a little strip of sky at the zenith. The trees were old twisty-rooted things with moss dangling from their branches and vines roping around their trunks. It was the kind of woods you felt might close over you if your back was turned. *Soon we shall plunge into the shadows cold*, he recited to himself.

The wind coming into the car had a different smell now, too. Rot and decay and the mossy smell of reptiles. A green wind, a wind that gave out a warning. The ravens had been replaced by egrets and herons, which broke from the woods and flew in startled packs across the two-lane highway.

A few miles later a sign told them they had entered

11

the Ocala National Forest. They were in the hammocks now, in the wilds. Neil also noticed they hadn't passed a billboard, or a gas station or any other sign of civilization, for the last forty minutes. He was glad he'd filled the tank back in Ormond. Every mile or so there was an emergency call box for motorists to use, which was more frightening than reassuring. It meant you'd have to phone for help, because there was no help around.

"We left Ormond exactly one hour ago," David said, looking at his watch. "Where's the magic road?"

"Stay calm," Randy said, without turning around. "Probably any minute now."

"Maybe we passed it already," Terry said. "This is really heavy woods, isn't it?"

Just as he said it, they entered a corridor of trees whose branches reached out over the road like broken fingers grasping at the car. The woods were so dense now you couldn't see the hills beyond them. Neil struggled to stay calm, because he knew for a fact he was the only calm one in the car.

"I'll bet we're lost," David said.

"There's no way to be lost," Randy snapped. "We took a road that runs straight from Ormond Beach to the other road we need. How could we mess that up?"

"We might have gotten off Route 40 somehow," David said. "Maybe there was a fork or something we didn't realize. I haven't seen any signs lately."

"I have a real serious question to ask," Terry said in a small voice. "What if somebody has to go to the bathroom?"

Neil laughed, glad for comic relief. "Does somebody have to go to the bathroom?" he asked, glancing around.

Terry had turned a deep shade of pink. "Did your cousins say anything about a rest stop anywhere near the cave, Randy?"

"Cross your legs!" David said. "This trip is taking too long as it is! I want to get to the goddamn cave while I'm still young enough to enjoy it!"

"I'm sorry," Terry said, shifting around. "But I don't think waiting would be a good idea."

"Stop the car and let him out!" Randy bellowed. "It's bad enough to have babies along without one of them wetting himself!"

"I really can't help this!" Terry pleaded. His voice carried an edge of hysteria. Neil stopped the car.

Terry opened his door and got out in slow motion, looking fearfully at the gnarly, tangled woods. "Anybody else want to come?" he asked.

"This isn't a trip to the powder room, Gladys!" Randy said. "Hurry up and do it!"

Terry stayed where he was, though, holding on to the car door. "I think I have another problem," he said.

Randy slid down low in his seat, exhaling loudly. Neil knew part of what was bugging Randy was the need to get moving and find out if he had gotten them lost in the wilderness.

"What's your other problem, Terry?" Neil asked.

Terry looked dangerously close to tears. "I don't want to go into those woods by myself," he said. "But I can't do it here in front of you guys either."

Randy appeared to explode. His arms and legs all splayed out at once. "Oh, for *Christ's* sake!"

"Nobody's going to watch you, kid," Neil said. "It's not that much of a novelty."

"Even if you didn't watch, I just don't think I could. . . . Do you think there are wild animals in these woods?"

"Just bobcats," Randy said. "And by the way, they're attracted to the scent of human urine."

"You're not helping!" Neil cuffed him gently. "Terry, come on. Either go up in the woods and do it or get back in the car and hold it. We can't mess around like this for you."

Terry looked fearfully at the woods. Then, with equal fear, he looked at the carload of impatient boys.

David got out of the car. "Look. Let me go with you. I won't listen and I'll turn my back."

"We should have seen this coming," Randy said to Neil from the side of his mouth. "This is probably something they planned."

David seemed to fly around the car to Randy's passenger window. He grabbed the bigger boy by the front of his sweatshirt with both fists and glared into his eyes. "Look, you! Enough is enough! Okay? I'm just trying to help him, which is more than anybody else here is willing to do!"

"I can go by myself!" Terry cried. "I'm fine!" He sprinted off and disappeared among the trees.

Randy, meanwhile, was in the last stages of self-control. "Tell your brother to let go of my fucking shirt," he said to Neil through his teeth.

"Let go," Neil said to David. "Randy didn't mean it. He was joking."

David released Randy roughly. "Some of your jokes aren't funny!" He stalked around the back of the car to his own side.

Randy swiveled with him, dark eyes narrowed to slits, every muscle of his body tensed with unspent anger. Neil didn't want to think what would happen if the two of them ever really had a fight. Neither one had any control when he lost his temper.

"Listen, Randy," Neil said. "It's fine to pick on the kids but let's lay off the homo jokes, okay? We have a long day to get through."

Randy sat back. "We'll see."

Neil sighed.

After a few seconds Terry came jogging out of the woods, looking happy and relieved. "Piece of cake!" he reported. "There was a moth but I faced him down. And look what I found!" He held up a little wildflower he'd picked, a delicate bell-shaped purple thing. "Isn't that pretty?"

Neil looked quickly at Randy. Randy smiled back and turned around to Terry. "Let's see it," he said. "Maybe we can figure out what it is."

Neil started the engine again. Five minutes later they reached Old King's Road, left the highway and began looking for the cave.

TWO

Once they were on the right road, the boys still had the challenge of finding the cave. Randy's cousins had left very vague instructions, using landmarks like "pine tree" or "bend in the road," which were useless. By ten-thirty they had stopped the car in three different places and hiked around three different rock formations, none of which had any entrances. The autumn sun had burned a hole in the clouds and was now glaring like a spotlight in the white sky, making them sweat under the straps of their backpacks.

To compound matters, David had picked up the scent of Randy's tension and was making little comments like, "It might be faster if we just dig our own cave." So far, Randy hadn't lashed out at David, but the potential, Neil knew, was growing. *Just please let us get to the goddamn cave,* he thought as they trudged and sweated and grumbled, *so I can go back to being the one in charge.*

Only Terry Quinn seemed to be having a good time, turning and swiveling his head to look up into the trees, pausing to listen to birdcalls, sometimes sprinting ahead of the others like a puppy and then waiting, bent over and panting, for them to catch up. Neil envied him.

"I know this is going to be it," Randy said for the fourth time as they approached an outcropping of golden-red stone in a grove of scrub pines.

Neil allowed himself some hope, too. This was a bigger formation than the others, maybe the size of a department store, rising like castle towers from a short, grassy hillside.

"If it's not, I say we eat our goddamn lunch, find some girls and get down to business," David said.

Terry giggled.

Randy had stopped speaking to David twenty minutes ago, so he addressed all his remarks to Neil. "They said you veer around to the right. . . ." He gracefully scaled the hillside and began to veer, grazing the stones with the flat of his hand.

Neil followed him up the hill. Randy's long wiry body was always a joy to watch in motion, especially at times like this, when he was charged up with feelings. Neil realized the entire expedition had been like one of their basketball games. When the score was uncertain, Randy was always tight and compressed, holding in something that looked like rage or maybe terror, but in the final five minutes, if it was clear they would win, Randy would seem to spring open like a jack-in-the-box, his arcs and jumps suddenly balletic. When Randy scored the last points of the game, as he often did, his final leap to the basket was as thrilling as a bird taking wing.

The younger boys also seemed to respond to the change in the air and scrambled up the hill.

Randy was moving fast, sensing something. His palm skidded over the jagged rocks as he broke into a trot, glancing back at the others in overheated triumph. They rounded one more bend and all stopped dead.

The opening was there, a doorway of darkness in the rocks. Aladdin's treasure cave flashed into Neil's mind. The next moment he thought of Darby O'Gill and the cave that could close up and trap you forever.

Randy's chest rose and fell rapidly. A single drop of sweat trickled along his cheekbone. "We did it!" he puffed.

"*You* did it," Neil said, knowing Randy was low on strokes. He offered the palm of his hand, which Randy slapped rather painfully. Then Neil turned his attention to the younger boys, realizing that they had not made a sound for several seconds.

Terry and David had drawn together and were standing shoulder to shoulder, staring into the mouth of the cave with almost identical expressions. Neil had seen this look on David's face before—standing on the high dive his first time, paralyzed and refusing to jump.

"This is a little scary," Neil said, to get it out in the open.

"Yeah," Terry said immediately.

"Why?" Randy cried. "Five hundred million people have gone in and out of this cave over the millennia and nothing happened to them!"

"You don't know that," David said.

"Well, come on," Neil said. "We have to go in after

18

we've spent all this energy getting here. If we see the rotted bones of other foolhardy men, we'll turn around and come back."

Randy flashed him a smile, dropped into a squat and unzipped his backpack, drawing out a long-handled flashlight. He aimed it at the rock face and flicked it on and off.

Neil followed suit. Slowly David did the same. Terry didn't move.

"What's wrong?" Neil asked. "Are you still scared?"

"Yes," Terry said, laughing nervously. "But that's not the problem. I didn't realize I'd need a light. I don't have one."

Randy drew in a sharp breath to say something, but David managed to cut in first. "That's okay. I brought two. And I have extra batteries in here if somebody runs out."

"Aren't you the little Eagle Scout!" Randy said. He peered at David's backpack, which did look very heavily loaded. "What have you got in there, boy? It looks like a goddamn hardware store."

David's blue eyes lifted, level and icy with pride. "Food, water, flashlights, batteries, Sterno, matches, a warm-up jacket, cap, gloves, a first aid kit, a Swiss Army knife, two hundred feet of nylon line and a collapsible shovel." He extracted a Dolphins cap and centered it over his blond forelock. "Okay?"

"Jesus!" Randy said. "All I've got is lunch and my flashlight and a rope. Maybe we should do a little inventory. What's everybody else got?"

"Just lunch," Terry said. "I guess I'm really stupid."

19

"I've just got food and water," Neil lied. No way to explain bringing a book of poems into a cave. "So don't feel bad."

Randy stood up, shouldering his pack. "Yeah, David's the freak here. What happened to you in a past life that you're so hyper? You must have been in a major disaster!"

Neil sucked in his breath, choked and started coughing. Terry, who also knew the story, whipped around to look at David.

Only David's eyes had changed. The pupils were narrowed to pinpoints. "Is that supposed to be funny, Isaacson?"

Neil struggled to talk between coughs. "He doesn't know," he choked out.

"I don't know what?" Randy tugged the strap of Neil's canteen, prompting him to drink.

Neil's esophagus wasn't being cooperative. He sipped and choked, desperate to be able to talk and take control of this horrible turn of events.

"David was in a disaster," Terry said to Randy. "Their house burned down two years ago."

Neil felt a heavy pressure in his chest. *Let's just go home,* he thought. *What's the point of anything?*

"Two years ago?" Randy said. "That's when I moved here."

Through Neil's watery eyes, David appeared to have turned to stone and was staring blankly at the woods. Neil took a final drink, then spoke. "It was the summer before you moved here. It burned"—he cleared his throat—"to the ground. We lost every-thing. He barely got out with his life. Mom and Dad and I were all away from the house when it hap-pened." Neil could hear his own voice careening up and down the scale as he skirted around the central fact of the tragedy.

Terry had been edging toward David, watching him carefully. He reached out now and brushed David's shoulder with the tips of his fingers.

"Take your *hands* off me, you fag!" David shrieked. His voice echoed through the trees. He turned away for a second, then sprinted off, around a bend in the rocks where they couldn't see him.

Neil let a few seconds go by, then turned to Terry, who was shaking, his hand still suspended in the air. "He didn't mean that," Neil said.

Terry let his hand fall. "I know."

"I didn't mean to upset him," Randy said quietly. He turned to Neil. "I mean, I didn't know. And why didn't I know? This is a small town! This is a big thing! Does everyone at school know about this?"

"I don't know. Probably. My parents talked to our teachers and I think everybody agreed it would help us if we could just forget this and put it behind us. A lot of people wanted to do things . . . raise money or give us things, put it on the local news. . . . Mom . . . . we couldn't stand that idea. We just wanted to put it all back together."

Randy frowned. "I'd think that would make it seem more weird. You just went back to school that fall and no one said a word to either of you?"

"Pretty much." It did sound a little strange now. But Neil could remember the hushed family discus-sions where everyone was in total agreement. Heads down, nodding, eyes darting around. *We've got to move on.* It was the only option besides going crazy.

Randy lowered his voice even more. "Was the fire David's fault?"

"Yes," Neil looked down to make sure the ground wasn't shifting.

Randy sat on a rock, hunched over, elbows on knees. "I'm really, really sorry. I guess we should just go home if David's this upset."

Neil sat down, too. "Give him a minute. Let's see what he does."

Terry sat down and began fiddling with his backpack.

A few seconds passed. Neil was aware of the woods: the scent of dry pine needles, the sandy texture of the soil beneath his hands, the way the wind was gently tossing his hair, the rising and falling drone of cicadas. Slowly he traced his initials in the dirt.

"I don't understand why you never talked about this, at least to me," Randy insisted. "I thought we were friends, you know?"

Neil knew. He thought of all the secrets he'd forced Randy to confess to him. "I don't know. Maybe I was glad you didn't know. That way, I didn't have to think about it when you were around, you know? It's funny the stuff I went through to hide it from you. When you first came to town, we were still living in a hotel on the beachside, waiting for the insurance money so we could buy a new house. You kept having me to your house and you were hinting all the

22

time you'd like to come to my house? And I'd always put you off?"

"I remember."

"I just didn't want you to know anything. It was six months before you met my family. I wondered what you were thinking."

Randy smiled crookedly. "I thought it was because I was Jewish."

"Oh!" Neil felt like he'd just taken a punch. "Oh, god!"

"It's okay. I'm glad that's not true. I've worried about it sometimes. Look, should we round up the kid and go home? This cave will still be here in another million years when David's feeling better."

Neil considered. "Can we wait a second? He really wanted to do this and he . . . I think he'd feel worse if we pulled the plug just because he lost it. He's pretty resilient."

They lapsed into another silence. Neil stared at his initials, looking for clues. When he raised his head, he saw that Terry was staring at him, questioningly. He looked away. Terry knew the whole story of the fire and must have been wondering why Neil still hadn't told Randy everything.

After a few seconds David's angular shadow stretched around the curve of the rocks, with David following. He looked a little stiff, but that was all. Neil could see he hadn't cried. When David cried, his fair skin got all red and blotchy. Neil could picture what David had probably done—stood there all alone with his whole body clenched, sobs detonating inside him, unable to batter their way out. David could be tough when he needed to, very, very tough.

"So," David said, "are we going into this goddamn cave or not?"

The other three stood in unison, hoisting up their packs and murmuring things like "Let's do it," and "Go for it." They turned their flashlights on and moved awkwardly forward. Neil automatically stepped through the cave mouth first, bowing his head and slicing the darkness with his frail beam of light.

———

At first the passageways were narrow, the ceiling so low everyone but Terry had to bend. Neil, who was six-three, had to bend over like a hunchback. They walked single file—Neil, Randy, David, Terry—each sweeping the walls and ground with his individual stream of light. Neil dragged his free hand across the dry, rough stone of the cave wall. The rock was the same dark gold inside as outside and felt like sandpaper. Occasionally the lights would pick up a vein of mica, glittering like a tiny galaxy in the darkness. The floor of the cave was hard-packed dirt with an occasional bony ridge of rock that would try to trip them or make them step up suddenly and bump their heads. There were no signs of life, no rustle of bat wings, no graffiti. The smell of old damp stone reminded Neil somehow of laundry detergent.

Neil hated being the leader, the first one to step into each new field of darkness. The other boys' lights crisscrossed and wove around him like searchlights, playing tricks with his vision. His chest, still sore from that coughing fit, seemed to be contracting, tightening down. He had the same kind of headache he often got from fluorescent lights. The worst sign of all, his unfailing signal that he was upset, had also surfaced. Passages from Baudelaire were flashing in his mind.

> *When earth is changed into a prison cell,*
> *Where, in the damp and dark, with timid wing*
> *Hope, like a bat, goes beating on the wall,*
> *Striking its head on ceilings mouldering;*

Neil remembered the stuck elevators in his past, the time he was twelve and the bolt on the men's room stall jammed and he started screaming instead of thinking to just slide under the door.

He remembered watching his sister's coffin go down into the ground, remembered the way his mother pulled at his arm because he couldn't seem to walk away from the grave.

He remembered last year when he and Randy had been involved in a practical-joke war. Randy had pushed Neil into a locker and slammed the door. When they let him out, Neil had jumped Randy like an animal, punching his face, drawing blood. Two assistant coaches had to hold Neil under a cold shower for ten minutes before the homicidal urges had passed.

None of these things had ever fit together in Neil's mind before, but now he could see they did, and there was a magic word that went with them. *Claus-trophobia*. To the others the cave was just a bunch of rocks. But Neil saw the cave as something that might be out to get them. It might want to trick them and trap them and hold them there. It might never let them go. He knew he was being crazy but he couldn't help it. Only one thing was really clear in his mind. This weakness had to be hidden from the others at all costs.

Neil picked up the pace of his stride a little, relaxing his muscles by sheer will. He was good at forcing his body to act at odds with his mind. In a few minutes he was loping along, graceful as a panther. Only his chest rebelled, drawing itself down tight, like a fist.

After a second, he realized he had been hearing Terry cough for the past few minutes. Grateful to have something besides himself to think about, Neil stopped and turned in the narrow space, shining his beam into Terry's face. Randy and David did the same thing, causing Terry to blink violently. As if he could hide his condition from them, Terry was clenching his jaw, which made each cough shake his whole body. His pony forelock had fallen down into his eyes.

"What's this about?" Neil asked gently.

Since he couldn't talk, Terry held out his hand to ward them off. He knelt on the cave floor and unzipped his backpack, rummaging until he found a silver-backed sheet of capsules. He popped one into his mouth, motioning for liquid. David gave him a box of apple juice.

"Now we find out," Randy said, trying to lean

against the curving wall. "We're in here with a junkie."

Terry's cough was subsiding. He giggled between sips. "I'm allergic to mold," he said. "But it's okay. I've got a lot of antihistamines."

Randy shook his head, laughing. "Oh, boy! What else, Terry? Let's have it all at once. Do you get hives? Incontinence? Seizures?"

Terry finished his juice slowly. "Well . . ."

"Do you believe this?" Randy asked Neil. "Do you believe this?"

"Terry," Neil said. "I really think you should come clean before we go any further. If you've got a heart condition or a brain tumor or something, we should know it right now. None of us are paramedics." Neil realized he was hoping Terry did have some kind of medical problem. Then they could call this whole thing off and no one would ever know how scared he had been.

"It's not a big deal," Terry said. "It's just going to sound like a big deal."

Randy squatted in front of Terry, looking into his face. "Spill it, junior. We want your full medical history now or you're going to be drinking your apple juice in a real funny way."

Neil glanced at David. David looked away.

"I have asthma," Terry said. "It comes and goes, but a situation like this might set it off—"

"No kidding!" Randy cried. "You little jerk! You're in a cave! You shouldn't be here at all! Damn it! Now we have to abort this whole thing for you!"

Neil closed his eyes. *Thank god.*

27

"No, we don't," Terry said. His round eyes were pleading. "Really we don't. I've got an inhaler. And I brought a canister of oxygen, just in case."

"Oxygen?" Randy squeaked. "Jeez! What else? You've probably got a wooden leg and a glass eye! This is too much." He looked up at David. "I'll bet you knew all this, too."

David shifted his weight to the other leg. "I know he has asthma. But Terry can handle it. He doesn't even get attacks that often."

"But we're in a *cave*," Randy said with exaggerated patience. "Asthmatics do not belong underground." He turned to Neil. "Am I right?"

"Right," Neil said, averting his eyes from Terry's. "I'm sorry, kid."

Terry slowly crushed his empty drink box into a ball, compressing it with both hands. Then he put it away in his backpack as if it were a valuable artifact. "I'm sorry," he said softly, keeping his eyes down. "I'm sorry I ruined things for you guys. That's all I do, basically." He stood up and slung his pack over his shoulder. "This will teach you to be nice. Next time you'll know better than to let some little jerk like me come along." He turned around in the narrow space. His shoulders, rounded in defeat, looked small and helpless.

"Wait," Neil said. His chest, which had just re-laxed, began to tighten again.

"Don't," Randy said to Neil. "Just for once, don't be a softhearted idiot. This isn't safe and we can't do it. I'm sorry, Terry, but you know I'm right."

"He's breathing fine now," David pointed out, looking hopefully at Neil.

Neil took a deep breath. "I think it's up to the person involved to decide what he can handle. If Terry thinks he's okay, then . . . he's okay."

"Bad call," Randy said, folding his arms.

Terry had turned back around and was staring at Neil. His eyes were moist with gratitude. "I know, I absolutely know I'll be all right. I swear I will."

"He swears, Randy," Neil joked weakly. "What more do you need?"

Randy sighed and hefted his pack. "I need to think that I'm in this cave with at least one other sane person. But I see that's not how it is. Okay. Come on. Let's go before we hear somebody's going into labor."

Neil turned back toward the darkness. The passage ahead looked just a little narrower, he thought. He put his free hand higher on the cave wall as he moved forward. Just in case the ceiling was getting any funny ideas.

THREE

The cave was larger and more complicated than Neil had imagined. Without flashlights, they would have been in total darkness. As they continued to explore, he noticed that the stone under his hands had become smoother and cooler. He wondered if David, who wore cutoffs and a tank top, was getting chilly. The air around them carried a new smell, something like musty apples. Other tunnels branched off from the main one— sometimes there were forks. Randy said they needed to bear right. His cousins had done so and found a spectacular vaulted chamber with calcite formations and crystals and a pool at its center.

But Neil had a bad feeling about it. Did Randy's cousins remember every single turn and twist they had taken? For that matter, how did they know for sure they were in Randy's cousins' cave? There had been no signs or markings outside. Maybe there were two thousand caves in this part of the forest. Maybe they were in a cave that was known to be unsafe.

The tunnel they were in now was larger. Neil

could stand up straight without bumping anything. However, he could feel in his calves that they were walking downhill. He wondered if they were below ground level. The thought made him edgy, brought funerals and graves back to mind. Moreover, he was hungry and tired and cold and he had to think about getting home in time for work at three o'clock, allowing for an hour's drive back to Ormond. Still, Neil didn't want to be the one to suggest they stop. His backpack felt heavy. The straps dug into his armpits. He wished Terry would have an asthma attack or something, but all the others seemed to be having a jolly time, shining their lights on the cave walls to look at fossils or veins of color, making jokes. Terry was humming to himself! Neil was appalled that in this group of relative misfits, he could possibly be the weakest link.

So he kept trudging, ignoring his sore calves, his cold hands and his empty, nervous stomach. He paid no attention to his Baudelaire flashbacks, which were growing more frequent with every step.

A cold sun hangs above for half the year,
And for the rest darkness covers all;
It is a land more barren than the Pole;
— No animals, or streams, or forests here!

Neil's hand grazed sticky, silken filaments. He ducked lower, wiping his palm on his jeans fast so the others wouldn't know a spiderweb could make him flinch. Nasty images filled his mind—the pale, blind cave spider falling into his clothes, pausing just for a second before it started crawling around. . . .

31

"Oh, gross!" Randy said. "Watch out, you guys, there's a big spiderweb up here. Yuck."

That's what a normal response sounds like. Gently Neil patted the front of his T-shirt to assure himself no one was taking a ride inside his collar. Very subtly he ran his hand through his hair.

"Is anybody getting hungry besides me?" David called.

"Yeah," Randy said. "But I was hoping we'd get to the big chamber by lunchtime. Then we'd have room to spread out."

We could go back outside! Neil thought. *Plenty of room to spread out under that big blue sky!*

"How you doing, Terry?" David asked. "Breathing okay?"

"I'm great!" Terry chirped. "Never felt better. Maybe this air is good for me."

Air? Neil thought. *What air?* The mustiness was increasing, filling his head with its fuzzy green funk. His breathing had become shallow. Lines of poetry flashed in his head like strobe lights. He hadn't felt this crazy since his sister's funeral. Then he began to sweat and shiver, as the cold air attacked his wet body. *I have to tell them,* he thought. *If I don't, I'll just start screaming and they'll know anyway.*

"You guys . . . ," he said, half turning.

A lot of things happened very fast. There was a sound like a sudden gust of wind hitting a palm tree. There was Randy, who had been looking at something on the floor of the passageway, suddenly looking up at Neil and shoving him forward so hard he

32

fell on his ass, a full two feet from where he'd been standing. His canteen smacked his face and his flashlight was knocked from his hand. He heard it rolling away. He turned back toward the others, outraged and confused, then saw the explanation for Randy's behavior framed in a pool of light from the other three flashlights.

There was a rattlesnake about ten inches from Neil's face as he lay there on the floor of the cave. Even allowing for his low angle and his terror, this was the biggest snake he'd ever seen in a lifetime of living in Florida. It was so big and so close, Neil could hardly take it seriously. It was like something in a Disney cartoon, coiled neatly with its two ends reared up. The rattle on its tail looked like some kind of plastic toy. The head was as big as a small cat's, hooded eyes glowering at Neil. All along its dark, shiny back was a delicate latticework of dusty-gold diamonds. Suddenly claustrophobia didn't seem like such a big deal.

The others had all stepped back to what looked like a safe distance. Terry whimpered involuntarily.

Neil heard himself laugh—a short, barking sound that echoed through the tunnel.

"Don't move," Randy whispered.

The snake swiveled its huge head, checking on the others, then returned its menacing glare to Neil. The tail made a little flourish, sending another rattle whispering through the silence.

I'm going to die, Neil thought. He wondered if the poison-sucking procedure from the old westerns really worked. Who would do it? David would. Maybe Randy. David had a first aid kit with him. Maybe it had some kind of antivenom in it.

Neil could smell the snake. It was an overpowering combination of stagnant water and raw liver. And he'd be willing to bet his own smell was just as repulsive to the snake, too. He noticed his hands, pressed against the dirt floor, were sweating so badly they created little spots of mud.

The worst thing was the way it stared right into Neil's eyes. Never in his life had Neil seen such intelligent, calculated hate. The scientists were wrong about reptiles and their brains. This thing hated him with a human, imaginative hatred. He could see it. He could feel it shimmering in the air between them.

"Neil?" Randy was saying softly. "We gotta do something here. I don't think you can safely move away, and even if you do, you're trapped on the wrong side of him. You can't risk trying to jump over him or going around him."

Yes, yes. Neil thought. *All true. None of it helpful. The solution is, this puppy is going to bite me and you kids are going to run like hell to get help before I die.*

The snake lowered its head. It had stopped rattling. Was that a good sign? Was it calmer now? Or was the rattle like Indian war drums? Did it stop just before the attack?

Neil tried to picture where the fangs would land. It could be the neck, the chest or the forearm, depending on the angle of the strike. All bad news. Too close to the heart. Randy had meant well by shoving him,

34

but it had been a terrible mistake. If he'd stayed on his feet, he'd have taken it in the ankle and he'd have a fighting chance.

The snake's head swayed lower, like a marionette on a slackened string. Neil felt he was beginning to sense its thoughts. "Keep your lights in his face," he whispered. "I think it's making him sleepy."

"Don't talk!" Randy whispered harshly. "Don't you move a muscle."

Neil looked up at them again. Randy seemed to have unwisely come forward a little. David looked paralyzed, his eyes staring vacantly, his flashlight arm unnaturally rigid. Terry was the worst. He was looking straight at Neil with tears running down his cheeks.

You little shit! Neil thought. *I'm not dead yet!*

Randy turned to David. "Listen. We have to do something. We could all go for help and hope the snake would move this way, to get away from Neil, but what if it didn't?"

"We can't go away," David said in a low, edgy voice. "We can't leave him."

"I think you're right," Randy said. "Because if the son of a bitch does bite him, we have to try and give him some kind of first aid right away. So . . ."

David's eyes finally left the snake and lifted to Randy's. "We have to kill it," he said calmly.

"No!" Terry's tone was high and childish. "What are you going to do? If you try to hit it with something and you miss, it'll go for Neil."

"Well, that's the chance we have to take," Randy

said. "If Neil moves, it's going to go for him anyway. He's got no way to get out of this cave unless we get this fucking viper out of the road."

"I brought a shovel," David said. "Remember?"

"Does it have a long handle?" Finally Randy's voice had begun to waver a little.

"Not really," David said grimly. He knelt down, slowly and fluidly, keeping his eyes on the snake.

It swiveled its head abruptly to see what the motion was about. On an impulse Neil decided to scoot away while the snake's attention was diverted. He slid about two inches before his enemy whipped around again. The rattle stiffened and chattered loudly.

"Don't move, you jerk!" Randy shouted.

The snake swung its head back toward Randy, rattling furiously.

"Don't shout, you asshole!" Neil whispered back. He had another one of those awful desires to laugh. The brain, he thought, was an interesting organ. Obviously he was going crazy and that was a blessing. Because he didn't really want to have all his faculties when that big, angry head came flying at his jugular vein.

David took a deep breath, clearly making a great effort to rise above the commotion around him. He unzipped his pack, slid the collapsed shovel out and rose in one, clean motion, locking the handle with the softest of clicks. His gymnast's muscle control and concentration were perfect in this situation. He could flow and be silent while the others' jerky movements definitely made the snake nervous. "I'll do it," he said softly to Randy.

"Uh-uh, Eagle Scout," Randy said. "I've got a longer reach than you. We need to have everything working for us here." He held out his hand for the shovel.

David didn't move. "I have to do it. He's my brother."

"Big deal. He's my best friend. And I've still got a longer reach than you, so that settles it."

David's eyes narrowed. "He's my brother," he repeated.

"He isn't going to be anybody's brother if you two don't quit acting like a Clint Eastwood movie and do something!" Terry said.

"I want Terry to do it," Neil whispered, giggling. "He's the one with the killer instinct." *Boy! I have gone right over the edge. I'm full-blown, batshit crazy!*

Randy extended his right arm across David's line of vision. It was an impressive arm, long and tan, the muscles compact and ropy. "See this? And I know I have good reflexes. Plus I'm a ruthless son of a bitch who loves to kill for pleasure. So give me the fucking shovel."

David's eyes were like ice chips in the dim light. "No."

Much as he was enjoying his vacation from sanity and responsibility, Neil saw that his leadership was needed. "Let Randy do it," he said to David. "I know how you feel, but I play ball with Randy and he's got quicker reflexes than anybody I've ever known. And he's six-one to your five-ten. He's probably got a two- or three-inch advantage over you, and right now that might count for everything.

37

You can save my life next time, I promise. Okay, Sport?"

Everyone, including the snake, was looking at David. The snake had been watching the other three boys ever since the shovel came out. Neil was tempted to try for a few more inches, but he didn't have the nerve.

David handed the shovel to Randy, scowling. "If you fuck this up and kill my brother, I'm going to bury this in your skull, Isaacson."

"Yeah, yeah, put it in your memoirs, Sonny." Randy took the shovel and played with his grip, like a golfer. "You guys keep your lights trained on Mr. Snake there. I don't want to lose him, okay? Neil, God help us both. When I count to three, you move, you move fast, okay?"

"Be careful how you swing," David fussed at Randy. "Don't lose your balance and fall right into him. And don't chop at him. You have to crush his brain. Try to bash his head against the floor. Or stun him the first time and then go for the kill."

"Write it all down for me," Randy said. "I'll read it later."

"Listen to him," Neil told Randy. "Everything he said was good. Especially that part about don't lose your balance. Believe me, you don't want to see this guy from the angle I've got."

"Don't worry. I'm not the self-sacrificing type. Do you think if I hold it up to aim it, he'll know what I'm doing?"

"Don't take the chance," David said. "You'll just

38

have to swing it up and down as fast and hard as you can."

"But I'm more likely to miss that way," Randy argued. "If I hold it up, he can fix his attention in this direction and Neil's got a better shot at moving away."

"No," David said. "The stupid thing is halfway calm now. If you raise that shovel in the air, he'll go on full alert. He might go crazy and strike at Neil. Just aim fast while you swing. You should be able to do that with your wonderful, famous reflexes."

"I sure am glad I went to the bathroom awhile back," Terry said.

"I wish I had," Randy said. He adjusted his grip once more. "Neil? On three. I hope snakes can't count."

Neil tensed all his muscles that were touching the floor. He had no urge to laugh or remember poetry now.

Randy closed his eyes briefly, as if praying. Then he looked at the snake, calm and focused. "One. Two. *Three!*"

Neil didn't try to see anything. He just scrambled blindly into the dark tunnel ahead, rolling painfully over his own flashlight as he heard a sickening thud, combined with a squishy sound, combined with a splintering, as if Randy had smashed a pile of Popsicle sticks. Or a small, fragile skull. Then there was the same sound a second time. And a third. Neil lay flinching in the darkness, sweating freely, his heart pumping so hard he could feel it in his brain. He wondered if Randy had needed to hit the snake three times or if he had killed it the first time and was now just venting his anger. He didn't want to know.

Silence. Neil lay still, soaked, chilled and panting. The lights all turned to him. He forced himself to sit up so they could see he was all right, even though he really just wanted to lie there awhile and marvel over the fact that he wasn't dead.

He slowly pulled his flashlight out from under his bruised thigh and aimed it toward the corpse of Mr. Snake, who still looked like a cartoon character in death, his head unnaturally flattened on the cave floor. A pool of bright red blood seeped around his huge jaws. It seemed horrible to think snakes had red blood just like people.

Above the kill stood Randy, in a cloud of slowly settling dust, his eyes still dark with whatever emotion he'd summoned to get the job done.

Strangely, Neil's first feeling was a kind of grief for the snake. He'd bonded with his killer in those close quarters. It was sad, he thought, that they'd blundered into Mr. Snake's world like this and forced him into a position where he had to die. The whole thing was sickening and wrong.

For a minute no one moved. Then Terry broke the spell, sagging against the wall, covering his eyes with his hands.

David suddenly ran foward, kicking the dead snake viciously out of his way. He threw himself down beside Neil, hugging him. "Oh, god!" he moaned.

Neil found this unbearable. "Cut it out." He pushed David's arms away. He stood up and left

David crouching there, walking over to Randy instead. They looked at each other and solemnly embraced. "Very nice job, teammate," Neil said.

"Just don't expect me to clean it and cook it for you," Randy said. He pulled back after a second, glancing in David's direction. Neil didn't look at David. He knew he'd hurt him, but shit, he'd just almost died. Wasn't he entitled to decide how he felt and who he wanted to hug?

Randy went to David and offered him a high five. "Way to go, Eagle Scout. Good man, bringing that shovel. If it wasn't for you, I'd have had to tie that sucker up with a piece of my rope!"

David slapped Randy's hand listlessly. "Glad I'm worth something here," he said quietly.

"Let's get out of here," Terry said. He was still keeping one eye on the snake, just in case. "Let's go find some nice Burger King where the french fries don't move or rattle."

"Maybe we *should* cut our losses here," Randy agreed. "I really don't feel like killing anything else today."

"Yeah," David said. "For all we know, Mrs. Snake and all the little snakes are just around the bend."

Neil reached down and picked up his pack, all his muscles complaining. "Randy, the next time you think of something exciting for us to do, remind me to kick your ass."

"Don't worry," Randy said. "That was all the excitement I need for ten years or so." He wiped his face with a bandanna and tied it around his forehead, Indian-style. There was a streak of dirt along one cheekbone. He looked like some kind of commando. "I think I need to take a souvenir from this," he said, bending to retrieve the shovel.

There was a chorus of *No!*'s, which Randy ignored as he raised the shovel again, swung and neatly chopped off Mr. Snake's rattle. He picked it up, wiped the remnants of blood on his jeans and tucked the rattle into his hip pocket. "Something to show the girls back home," he said, smiling.

Neil stood very still while an urge to vomit came and went. "Why don't you go first for a while, Mighty Hunter?" he said in a hoarse voice. "I've had enough of being the leader."

Everyone took one last look at Mr. Snake and slowly fell into formation. Randy led this time, going back the way they came. "Neil, drink some water," he said. "You were sweating like a pig back there and you might be dehydrated."

Neil was happy to oblige. In fact, once the water started flowing into his mouth, he couldn't have stopped anyway. It was the first sensation of comfort and wellness his body had felt in hours. The first of many, he promised himself. Soon they'd be seeing the sky again and feeling the warm sunshine. Soon he'd be dredging a handful of french fries in catsup. Tonight he'd be in a warm bed in a safe house, far from all the snakes in Florida.

Neil could feel the relief flooding his body, unkinking the muscles in his arms and legs like a hot whirlpool. He was getting out of this without losing face. And the great thing was, he knew none of these heroes would ever want to venture into a cave again.

42

He wondered if they would dare tell this story at school. The temptation would be great, especially for Randy, but if the story got back to any parents . . . well, it wouldn't be good. He couldn't imagine what his mother and father would say. The cardinal sin, for the past two years, was to take any kind of chance with your safety.

Randy stopped suddenly and David, who was behind him, bumped into him. They stood at a three-way fork of tunnels. "I don't remember this," Randy said softly.

Everyone stood very still, looking at the tunnels very hard. "Neither do I," said David.

"That doesn't mean anything!" Neil said. "A fork always looks different when you come at it from the other way. We were bearing right all the way in, so all we have to do is bear left all the way out!"

"Would that really work?" Terry said. "Because if there were channels feeding in to the right of us, which we didn't notice before . . ."

"What are you talking about?" Neil shouted. "We can't be lost! I have to be at work by three o'clock!"

"Hey, hey." Randy inserted a hand between Neil and Terry. "Calm down, Neil. I think your adrenaline is stuck from the snake episode."

No buddy. This is all new adrenaline. Because I know we'll never get out of here and you're about to hear me screaming like you've never heard me screaming before.

"You know what?" David said. "We should have left marks or dropped a trail of something on the way in here."

"Very brilliant, thinking of that now," Neil said.

"Well, you didn't think of it either!" David shouted back.

"You guys!" Terry wailed. "You don't think we're *lost*, do you?"

"No!" Neil said. "These guys are just freaking out. They're the ones with stuck adrenaline. We're going to go left at this fork and every other fork and we'll be out of here in a few minutes. Here, let me go first again. This group is unstable with you at the helm, Randy." Neil pushed past the others and took the left tunnel without looking back, driving himself forward with hard, aggressive steps. He could hear the others falling into formation behind him.

12:30 P.M., SATURDAY

Ten minutes later, they came to a tunnel where someone had written RICK on the wall with something soft and black, like charcoal. All four boys came to a complete stop. Their collective breathing echoed.

"If we'd gone past that before, somebody would have seen it," David said. He adjusted the visor of his cap and turned to Neil.

"Right," Neil said. His body felt like a stone falling through water.

Randy threw back his head and shouted. "Hey, Rick! How do you get out of here?"

Nobody laughed.

"How long does it take before people starve to death?" Terry asked Neil.

"That's not funny, Gingerbread," Randy said.

Terry turned to him. "I want to *know*."

Neil sat down in the dirt, propping his wrists on his knees. His hands dangled like dead fish. "It takes weeks to actually starve," he said. "But if you don't get water, you can die in like a couple of days."

David sat down opposite Neil. He scooted one

45

foot forward so the toe of his sneaker grazed the toe of Neil's sneaker. Neil's mind flashed to their childhood, when David was a toddler. They sat together at the dining room table and David would prop one little foot on the edge of Neil's chair. "You know what I read somewhere?" David said. "I read that if you're in a situation where there's no water, you can drink your own piss. Some guys on a raft did that."

Randy rested his back against the cave wall and slid down into a crouch beside David. "Be my guest, Nature Boy. As for me, I think some fates are much worse than death."

David frowned at him. "I just think we should look at every possible angle. That's what people in these situations do. I mean, no matter how big or confusing this cave is, if we keep looking long enough, we're bound to find the way out. But we don't know how long that will take and we don't have a lot of supplies so we have to think how we'll keep going."

Neil felt the funniest urge to go to sleep. When he spoke, his voice was low and tired. "My canteen is empty. How much stuff do we have to drink?"

"I've got five boxes of apple juice and a full canteen of water," David said.

"Nothing," Terry said, looking down.

Randy smiled crookedly.

"People need a gallon a day to survive," David said. "I remember that from the hurricane."

"Well, I'm glad we did that little calculation," Randy said. "We'll be dead by three o'clock, then."

"Aren't caves supposed to have a lot of water in them?" David asked Neil.

"Why do you always turn to me like I know everything!" Neil snapped. He pulled his foot away from David's.

"Yes," Randy said to David. "Caves are supposed to be pretty wet, the way I understand it."

"Thank you," David said, sliding his eyes toward Neil.

"I'm sorry," Neil said.

"Forget it," David said. "You will, anyway."

Terry sat down on David's other side, hugging his knees. They all faced Neil like a jury. "This conversation is making me thirsty," he said, tossing his hair out of his eyes.

"Oh no it isn't!" Neil said. "From now on, we're on rations!"

"That's fine for you!" Terry said. "You just drank a whole canteen by yourself!"

"Excuse me!" Neil shot back. "When a fucking rattlesnake almost bites you and you sweat like a horse, you can have a drink, too!"

"Neil, chill out," Randy said softly.

"Fuck you!" Neil said. "Fuck all of you!" His voice echoed up and down the tunnel.

"You guys," David said. "One thing's for sure. We aren't going to find water or the way out if we sit here on our asses yelling at each other." He stood up and hoisted his pack.

"Yep." Randy slid back up the wall, smooth as a shadow.

Terry stood up, too. "Which way do you want to go, Neil?"

Now they're patronizing me, Neil thought. He felt

47

like a child down on the ground with all of them standing over him. *This is not good at all. I have to calm down.* Neil took a deep breath and stood up. "Let's go back the way we came for a while. That would be the general direction we started in and that, theoretically, is where Randy's imaginary cousins saw the imaginary pool of water. And since we have absolutely nothing else to cling to for hope, we might as well go with that."

Randy grinned, slinging his backpack up. "Sounds like a plan to me." He put his hand on David's shoulder. "Hey, Eagle Scout. Why didn't you think of a compass? If we had a compass, we'd only be half as lame as we are now."

"If we killed you and drank your blood, we wouldn't be thirsty and it would be twice as quiet," David replied.

Randy laughed.

They began to trudge again.

"That was a joke, right?" Terry said to David. "I mean, I saw that TV movie about those people in the mountains in California. Did anybody see that? I mean, no matter how desperate we get, we wouldn't eat each other, would we?"

"Don't say anything, Randy," Neil said without looking around.

Randy snickered. "I think they always eat the smallest and weakest, first. Don't they, Terry?"

"I think they take a vote," David said. "And whoever's pissing everybody off the most gets to be the appetizer."

Everyone was quiet for a while after that.

Neil heard a sound in the distance. For a second he thought he was going crazy. It sounded like a little girl, laughing. He kept it to himself for a few more steps until the sound was clearer, and then he turned to David. "Stop," he said. "Listen."

It was water, running water, echoing back through the tunnels. It was as exciting as hearing another human voice. Neil listened for direction, then aimed his light toward a left fork. "This way," he said.

Two steps into this tunnel, his light picked up shiny ribbons of water seeping down the cave walls. "Look!" he cried, running his fingers through the dribbles. "We're in a wet place!"

"Keep going." Randy nudged Neil with his flashlight. "The sound is getting louder."

It was. A steady, musical ripple of sound, like bells or chimes or a distant, rolling fire. Neil felt almost dizzy with joy, which he knew was crazy. Finding the way out would be exciting. This was just a drink of water. But he felt as if someone had just let him into the bank vault and told him he could roll around in the money. The tunnel they were in now was so big they could walk two by two. The air around them was chilly. Water dripped from the high ceiling, splashing their faces like rain.

"Yes!" Terry said. He took a little jump in the air like a puppy playing in a sprinkler.

Neil broke into a jog.

Another bend and then the giggle of the water was a loud, raucous chuckle. The echoes of the cave made it sound like millions of little creatures laughing. Neil thought of *The Wizard of Oz*. They must be right on the source of it now. Neil aimed his light and found it. The other three lights followed.

There was a ledge of rock near the ground on the left wall. Water was arcing up from it like a drinking fountain, spilling down into a narrow stream that ran off into the tunnel ahead. Their flashlights made the water sparkle like liquid fire.

"What is that?" Terry said. "How did they get the water to do that?"

"It's a spring, you idiot," Randy said. He turned to the others. "Isn't it?"

"Well . . . yeah," Neil said. "Of course it is. I mean, I've never actually seen a spring. But this is what they do. Water jumping out of a rock is a spring. So I guess we have our own Perrier here."

Randy opened Neil's backpack, took out the empty canteen and knelt on the wet slippery rocks, like a pilgrim at a shrine. "God loves us," he said. "I knew it all along."

"Wait!" David said. "You don't know it's safe."

Neil wanted to pick up a rock and hit him in the head. "It's *spring* water, David! It comes from the water table, just like a well that somebody would dig. It's standing water that's not safe, right? But water like this is probably cleaner than the tap at home!"

"Where do you guys get all these facts you throw around?" Terry said. "Because I have a bad feeling most of your knowledge is from comic books and Rambo movies."

"Where else do you learn things?" Randy was stubbornly filling Neil's canteen. "If it weren't for comic books and Rambo movies, you'd have to depend on the crap they teach you in school."

Neil laughed. "But I'm right—right, David? I'm sure spring water is the best stuff."

David frowned. "Well, I think that's how it was before pollution, but now—I mean, how do we know this spring isn't running off some nuclear dump?"

The canteen was full. Randy pulled it out of the stream and looked at it. "We don't know," he said.

"So if it is, we can glow in the dark and save on batteries!" Neil said. "Jeez, what a bunch of pussies! We have to take some kind of risks here or we're going to die anyway. The bottom line is we need water for the rest of today and maybe for longer than that. And the only other option we've heard is David's stellar piss idea."

"Give me the nuclear runoff," Terry said.

"Look, here's what we'll do," Randy said. "We'll give Terry a drink and then watch him for the next couple of hours." He offered Terry the canteen.

To everyone's surprise, Terry shoved it away so hard it almost made Randy lose his balance. "I'm getting sick of you picking on me, okay?"

"Okay!"

"Here." David snatched the canteen out of Randy's hand, upended it and took five long swallows. He screwed the top on and wiped his mouth with his arm. "Watch me for the next few hours."

"David!" said Neil. "I can't believe you did that."

David shrugged. "Somebody had to. I didn't take all that much. If there's something wrong with the

51

water, I'll probably just get sick. It tasted good, though." He started walking.

Everyone fell in behind him.

———

The stream grew wider and wider, bubbling and foaming. It seemed like an entity to Neil—an over-excited guide eager to lead them somewhere, show them something.

The water took a wild slingshot turn and flowed through a wide doorway of stone. For a horrible, wonderful, thrilling, heart-stopping second, Neil thought they were looking at the way out, because there was light beyond the doorway. Natural light. Sunlight. David ran through first, the hair under his cap kindling from ash to gold. He skidded to a stop and arched his back, staring at something above him.

One by one they all followed and did the same, looking up and gazing. Then slowly their eyes swept down the walls and fixed on the floor at the center of the room.

They were standing inside a circular, vaulted chamber. The ceiling, Neil guessed, was about a hundred feet high. In the ceiling was a fissure, roughly the size and shape of a large ironing board. Beyond the fissure was the sky. The same sky that hung over the real, free world outside.

The weather had cleared since this morning and the sky was a rich crayon blue. The edge of a cloud showed, too. Bright white with a yellow rim where it caught the noonday sun.

The light fell in a wide shaft down into The Chamber, giving it an illumination equivalent to lamplight. Inside the light shaft, constellations of dust danced and swirled.

The walls of The Chamber were thickly layered with huge white calcite formations, tapering to bumpy points like giant candle drips. Up near the fissure in the ceiling were two fascinating things. On the left, a cluster of crystals lodged in the rock, as perfectly cleft and faceted as if a jeweler had cut them. They were some kind of quartz, Neil thought, white with an amber tinge that may have come from the sunlight hitting them.

On the other side of the fissure was a mass of black bats, hanging by their feet, as still as death, sleeping in the shade.

In places, the stalactites dripped puddles of water down onto the dirt and stone floor.

In the center of The Chamber, where the stream rushed to its conclusion, there was an almost circular pool of water, about six feet in diameter, which looked deep and still, even though a stream was pouring into it. A few bubbles broke on the surface every few seconds, sending out slow ripples. The cloud above the ceiling fissure was mirrored on the dark surface.

"Those holes where water sleeps," Neil recited to himself.

No one moved or spoke for a long time, listening to the stream rush into the muffling silence of the pool. Listening to the periodic drip of the calcite. Breathing the cool, cellar-smelling air. Neil didn't know what he was feeling. He didn't think he'd ever seen anything so beautiful in his life. But it was also a blind alley, a seductive trap. The sky mocked him, through that distant, unreachable window. Now they had a beautiful supply of fresh water to keep them alive and alert while they slowly starved. Was this an oasis, or just a comfortable, luxurious burial chamber? Still, there was something about the grandeur of it that made him feel safe. He remembered years ago, before the tragedy, when he used to look at sunsets and other majestic things and believe in God.

"Shit," Randy whispered. The susurration bounced like a gentle chime up the walls.

Then there was a different sound, an echoing whisper, a rustle of papers, an approaching train. The bats. Randy had awakened the bats, and they began to stir, first one, then a few, then all, restlessly taking wing and soaring in all directions, their darkness muffling the sunlight. Their hissing wing beats were amplified and multiplied by echoes.

Everyone below reacted the same. They all cursed, then crouched, covering their heads with their arms, peering up at the boiling black chaos in the sky.

Some of the bats flew out the ceiling opening. Some poured like a horde of demons through the doorway into the other cave tunnels. Two or three continued to career inside The Chamber, as if unsure what to do. Finally they scattered and the last echo died away into silence.

"God damn!" Randy said, getting up slowly. "I used to think I liked wildlife, but after today—"

"They won't come back, will they?" Terry asked. He still had his arms over his hair.

"Only after they're sure we're dead," David said grimly.

Dead, dead, dead, echoed the walls.

"Let's ban that word for a while, could we?" Neil said.

"Sorry, just kidding." David moved toward the pool. "Isn't this something?" He knelt at the edge of the water and peered in. "It's deep." He stuck in his arm and leaned, going all the way to his shoulder. "Way deep. And it's freezing cold. Isn't that strange?"

"Be careful," Neil said. "Don't fall in."

David sat back on his heels, shaking off his wet arm. "Like I can't handle myself in water!" His bookshelf at home was crammed with two years' worth of Red Cross awards and diving trophies.

Randy was circling the perimeter of The Chamber, like a dog marking territory. "This has to be the same place my cousins were talking about."

Terry took off his pack and sat on the ground. "So, good. I feel so much better. Now let's call them and ask them how they got out of here." He turned his round face up to the ceiling and the sunbeam illuminated him like a picture in a religious magazine. *The choirboy at prayer,* Neil thought. Then there was some very subtle change in Terry's expression. A narrowing of the eyes, a tightening of the jaw. Suddenly his mouth opened wide. "HEEEEEEEEEEEEEELP!" he screamed. "SOMEBODY PLEASE HELP US. PLEASE." His voice frayed into hoarseness. "Please. Please." His head lowered. His shoulders rounded and began to shake.

Meanwhile the walls were a step behind. HELPHELPHELPHELPHELP!

Neil put his hands over his ears. It was like hearing his own feelings leaking out.

David scrambled over to Terry. "Hey! Stop that. That's crazy."

CRAZYCRAZYCRAZY.

"There might be somebody out there," Terry choked out. "They might hear us. We have to get out of here. I want out!" He covered his face with both hands.

Want OUT.

David put a hand on Terry's shoulder. "It's okay. We all feel like that."

Neil's eye was drawn to Randy, who was moving toward David and Terry with increasing speed. He had a look of purpose about him. Neil had the terrible idea that maybe Randy was planning to slap Terry to his senses, like Patton and the crying soldier.

Meanwhile, Terry had completely crumbled. His forelock bounced over the hands shielding his face. "I'm sorry," he was gasping. "I'm a jerk . . . I can't . . ."

Randy was right on him now, standing directly behind him. His gaze was as focused as when he aimed at the snake. Randy went down on his knees behind Terry and wrapped both arms around him like a cocoon. "It's okay," he said. "Go ahead."

They were all three clustered together now. Only Neil stood apart, in the shadows.

Neil was shocked. This was the last thing he'd expected to see Randy do, but it had seemed like a natural impulse. Then Neil remembered that Randy had two younger sisters and that they'd all gone through a terrible divorce together. Maybe he'd been drying tears right and left the past few years.

David slowly withdrew his hand from Terry's shoulder. He was also looking at Randy in amazement.

Neil realized he was trembling and didn't know why. This should have been a nice moment but he felt . . . almost angry. Tremors ran up and down his legs.

He looked down and saw he had wrapped his arms around himself and was imitating Randy's hug to the letter. A big jerk trying to comfort himself, in the dark where no one could see.

F I V E

Neil stepped out of the shadows. "Come on, guys," he said. "This isn't working. I mean, you all get the part and everything, but this is not the Hallmark Hall of Fame. We've just fucked up and all we have to do is unfuck ourselves, which we are going to do. Am I right?"

All of them, even Terry, laughed a little. Randy let go of Terry's shoulders. The three of them formed a line on the ground, turning their faces up to Neil.

This is the way it should be, he said to himself. *Team and captain. Even if the captain doesn't have a clue what to say next.* "So we're a little scared," he began. "We thought we would breeze in, piss on some rocks and breeze back out. And now we're lost and we don't exactly know how to find our way back. My point is, it's *normal* to be a little scared. But if we look at the real facts in a rational way, the situation is not that bad."

He paused, in case one of them wanted to jump in with some of those rational facts. He personally couldn't think of any.

58

"My cousins are idiots and they found their way out," Randy offered.

"Good point!" Neil cleared his throat. "So . . . the fact is, there's nothing to panic about. We saw this cave from the outside. We know its size. It just isn't that big. So we know if we make a good effort, we can definitely find the way out. What we need, I think, is some kind of good trail-marking system, so we don't keep doubling back over the same ground, and also so we can always get back to this water source if we need to. So help me think. Other than food, which we need to conserve, what have we got that we can use to mark a trail?"

David was already rooting in his pack. He set the first aid kit out. "Let's see what's in here. I've also got a knife, which we might use to scratch the rocks, but that wouldn't be very visible and it might wreck the knife, which we might need."

"Why do you think we're going to need a knife?" Terry asked, grabbing David's arm.

Randy answered him. "In case the next thing we see, instead of a snake, is a wildcat or a serial killer with a hockey mask. Look in the first aid kit, David. There's probably iodine or something."

Neil thought of his book. If they couldn't find anything else, they could tear up little pieces of paper and leave a trail. He almost laughed, picturing some new group of kids exploring the cave and finding a little scrap of paper that said, for instance, *I am a boudoir full of faded flowers*.

"Betadine," David said, holding it up. "Four bottles with little applicators. Obviously a sign from God."

"Only if it leaves a stain on rock," Randy said. "If it doesn't, it's an up-yours from God."

David got up and went to a wall, where he neatly lettered DAVID ROBERT GRAY in dark, rusty letters that stood out sharply against the grayish rock. Neil thought it looked almost like dried blood.

"Perfect," Neil said. "Okay, here's the plan. Let's eat something. I think half the reason we're all going crazy is we're just hungry and tired. After lunch we need to split up and start searching and marking. Sooner or later, one of us will exhaust all the stupid possibilities and find the way out. In fact, he might find some *other* way out."

"That's right!" David said eagerly. "Wow, I never thought of that! Our odds might be better than we thought."

"Right," Neil said, feeling really good for a second. "Anyway, that person follows his trail back and finds everybody else."

"No!" Randy said. "That person gets the Sheriff's Department and the Park Service and the Red Cross and Batman and Robin and John Rambo and all the Ninja Turtles to come back here and find everybody else. There's strength in numbers."

"And the park people might have maps to these caves," Terry said.

Neil knew they were right, but he didn't like it. What if he wasn't the first one out? What if there were more snakes or extremely narrow tunnels? He didn't like the idea of being alone at all. "Yeah," he said.

"I think we should write our initials every few

yards," Terry said. "So, like if everybody except Randy gets out, we can pick up the trail that says RANDY."

"That's good," Neil agreed. "That's *very* good thinking." He turned to David, who had been quiet. "Anything else?"

David shifted the little bottles like chess pieces. "I'm tired of always being the one who thinks of all the negative stuff," he murmured.

Neil sighed. "We're tired of it, too. But we'd better hear it."

David dragged a bottle slowly through the dirt, like a toy truck. "Well, this is a good plan and I think it will work, but the only thing we haven't thought of is what if this cave has tunnels that don't show from outside that go on for miles and miles?"

Neil rubbed his forehead. "Yeah, that's a possibility. But if that's true, there's nothing we can do about it. So there's no point in bringing it up, right?"

"Yes there is," David said. "If we look all day and no one finds the way out, we have to come back here where we can at least have water and some fresh air."

"And each other," Terry said quietly.

"And each other. The point is, we have to set a time when we give up for the day today."

"No!" Neil's voice bounced up and down the walls. "We don't need to do that. That's just defeating ourselves before we start!"

Randy laid a hand on Neil's arm. "Hey. Don't get angry. He's right. We have to be practical. Otherwise some hero type, I won't name any names, will kill himself refusing to give up."

61

Neil sighed and looked at his watch. "I hate all of you. Especially when you're right. Okay. It's a little after one now." A brief picture of his mother flashed into his mind, standing in the middle of the kitchen, hands on hips, impatient with Neil and David for not letting her know they wouldn't be home for lunch. "We'll eat lunch and then start out. What's a reasonable time to quit? Five?"

"Four," said David.

"Five," said Neil. "An extra hour could make all the difference."

"Or if we run out of stuff," David said. "I don't know how long each bottle will last. If anyone starts to run out of Betadine, he automatically has to come back here."

"Check," said Randy. "Now let's eat. I'm starving."

David pulled a crumpled jacket from his backpack and spread it on the ground. It was his navy blue warm-up from the diving team with SEABREEZE SAND-CRABS in big white letters. Everyone unloaded their food.

David had brought four sandwiches: sliced turkey on whole wheat neatly folded in waxed paper and packed in a Ziploc. He also had an orange, a bunch of celery sticks—David believed in proper nutrition—and a whole box of Cinnamon Teddy Grahams. There were five containers of apple juice left from his original six-pack.

Neil had a large box of Triscuits, a Ziploc with a handsome wedge of cheddar cheese—not the low-fat junk his mother bought but the good stuff from his private stock—two Granny Smith apples and two

Mars bars, none of which, he realized, he wanted to share.

Randy, who didn't believe in proper nutrition, had a family-size bag of Doritos Cool Ranch Flavor, a Tupperware container of leftover fried rice and two Boston cream doughnuts.

Terry had three peanut butter and jelly sandwiches, a large bag of Cheez Doodles and a dozen of his mother's oatmeal Scotchies, minus the four they'd eaten in the car.

"Thank god we're all pigs!" Randy said, when it was all spread out on the jacket. "Finally we did something right!"

"What we need to do," David said, "is eat the most perishable stuff first. So that would be my sandwiches and Randy's doughnuts. Everything else we should save."

"Won't those candy bars melt?" Terry asked, ogling Neil's chocolate.

"Not in a cave," David said. "Is there meat in the fried rice?" he asked Randy.

"Nope. My sister Chloe made it, and she's into some kind of Chinese-Indian-vegetarian thing. So it's just got tomatoes and carrots and stuff. It's really good, though. She uses hot peppers and all that. Blow your jets out."

The mention of Chloe's name made Neil's mind wander briefly. Sometimes, when all the stars were aligned correctly, Neil would go to Randy's after school and while Randy changed his clothes or took the dog outside for a few minutes, Neil would stroll, oh, so casually, into the Isaacsons' little kitchenette where Chloe would be, chopping and slicing, her small, curvy body packed into tight jeans and one of her famous scoop-neck T-shirts. The late afternoon sun would edge her dark hair with crimson, like the red glow inside Coca-Cola. Neil would study the pattern of freckles on the bridge of her nose or the curve of her dark eyelashes. Cooking was performance art to Chloe. She chopped like a murderer, ground fresh herbs with a mortar and pestle. Sometimes she would fling carrot chunks or onion slices in a high, thrilling arc across the kitchen, where they would splash like carp into a pot of boiling water.

In her presence, Neil felt as if old rusty bolts and latches inside him were breaking open, springing free. He had loved her since she was fourteen, when his lust had seemed dark and perverted to him, but now she was sixteen and he was seventeen, so things had moved into the realm of possibility. He was faithful to Chloe in all his fantasies, never cheating on her with Winona Ryder or Shannen Doherty. No one, in his mind, could compare with Chloe Isaacson, smoldering in that cramped kitchen like a little volcano. Sometimes Randy would bring her leftovers to school for lunch and Neil would trade anything to get them, cherishing the sting of her Tabasco on his tongue all afternoon.

As far as he could see, though, this great romance was all one-sided. When he did make these hopeful pilgrimages into the kitchen, Chloe behaved exactly as if a friendly but scruffy dog had wandered in. "Hi, Neil. How's it going? Want a carrot?" she'd ask, without even making eye contact. He knew he was invisible to her, just Randy's big, clumsy friend, who might track mud in.

Of course Neil never breathed a word of his feelings to Randy. It just seemed so smutty and . . . rude, going into a guy's house and then getting hot about his sister. Neil could remember how protective he'd felt toward Mimi and she'd only been nine when she died. Neil and David had automatically snarled at any little male friend she brought home, just as a matter of course. Just like you'd lock a door or look both ways when you crossed the street. He didn't want Randy to see him as that kind of threat.

This past year Chloe had really developed. Neil had begun to realize that, any day now, Randy would be telling little stories about Chloe and this or that acne-riddled sophomore. And Neil's dreams would be crushed.

Randy swatted Neil's arm so hard it felt like a burn. "Hey! Tune in, boy! People are talking to you!"

Neil blushed. For a second he'd thought Randy could read his mind. "What?" he said. "I'm sorry."

Randy looked at David. "Don't you hate it when he does that?"

"Yes! He does it on purpose, like when he's mad at me. He can just tune everything out."

"He's a radio head," Randy agreed. "What channel were you on, Neil? Probably the women channel."

Neil hoped the soft light of the cave chamber distorted the color of his face. "No . . . I—"

"Never mind." Randy held up his hand. "We don't want to know your sexual fantasies anyway. We just want you to bless the food plan. We're going to eat the turkey sandwiches, divide up the doughnuts and each have an apple juice for vitamins. Okay?"

Neil struggled to concentrate. "No. The drink boxes are good forever if you don't open them. We should have fresh fruit. And oranges are more perishable than apples, so we'll split up the orange." *No one is touching my fucking apples until it's a matter of life or death.*

"Sounds like a plan to me." Randy stood up. "And here's a final housekeeping question. Where the hell is the boys' room? This stream, I assume?" He had already cocked his hips forward and was reaching for his fly. Randy wasn't known for modesty.

"No!" Terry screamed. "That's our drinking water!"

"It's running water," Randy argued. "And I've been holding it in for a good two hours now, so if we need a committee meeting, it better be fast." He kept his hand poised over his zipper, like a gunslinger, ready to draw.

"Terry's right," Neil said. "That water runs into the pool we might need for washing and stuff later on. We shouldn't contaminate it."

Randy straightened up. His dark eyebrows drew together slightly. "Listen here. I've been in a goddamn car for two hours getting here and then another I don't know how long wandering around. I killed a fucking snake for you. I'm not in the mood to stand here and explode while David builds us a men's room. So somebody point me in the direction you want me to go, because I'm going!" He arched his pelvis at the group.

"Go out and pick a tunnel near the spring and

66

that's what we'll all use. Mark it, so we'll know." Neil tossed the Betadine to Randy.

"We have a shovel," David said. "Should we dig a latrine?"

"I knew it!" Randy screamed. "He's going to want to put down a tile floor and hang guest towels while my kidneys go bankrupt!"

"Take the shovel and leave it there," Neil said. "We should bury everything because . . . well, in case we're here a while. But I don't think we need major construction."

"You're right," David said. "We'd starve to death before we'd go to the bathroom enough to justify a latrine."

"And on that happy note . . ." Randy shouldered the shovel like a rifle. "Don't talk about me while I'm gone." He sauntered off, tossing the Betadine bottle up and catching it.

Terry looked after him admiringly. "He's so cool. I wish I could just shrug things off like he does."

"Some of it's an act," Neil said.

"It's a good act!" Terry said.

"I think he's a pain in the ass," David said. "Everything's a joke to him."

"We're not supposed to talk about him," Terry said anxiously.

"*That* was a joke," Neil told Terry.

"That's what I mean," David said. "Why can't he just say, 'I'm going to the bathroom. Goodbye?' Would it kill him?"

"Why couldn't he be exactly like you and then he'd be perfect?" Neil said.

David tore open a sandwich. "I didn't say I was perfect! I never said that!"

"You act like you think you are." Neil realized he was deliberately picking a fight but he couldn't help it somehow.

"You're crazy!" David's pale eyes blazed.

"You wrap sandwiches perfectly, that's for sure," Terry said, applying his teeth to the waxed paper. "I can't get this open."

Neil laughed, but he felt cheated. He wanted to spar with David some more. Every once in a while this mood would come over him and he would get the urge to needle David into one of his frenzies. It was easy enough to do. A combination of sensitivity and rage like David's was a rare opportunity for anyone who wanted to get his or her hostilities out.

Randy came back and dropped into an Indian-style position next to Neil. "What'd I miss? Did David figure out that in a pinch we can cook and eat the rattlesnake?"

"Watch it," Neil said. "The kid is already pissed at you, Rand. He was shooting his mouth off about you when you were gone."

Randy's head came up fast. "Oh? What'd he say?"

"Nothing!" Terry cried. His sandwich hand shook slightly.

David was glaring at Neil. "What did you go and say that for? Are you trying to start something?"

Randy was slowly running his index finger around the tape on his sandwich, popping the seals one by one. "What's wrong, Davie? Do you only like to pick on me behind my back? Are you, maybe, *scared* to say something to my face?"

"Please, you guys," Terry begged.

"I said I wished you'd say something serious once in a while," David said evenly. "That's all."

Randy's eyes were slits. "Here's something serious. Stay out of my face, you little pretty boy, or I'll do you worse than I did the snake."

"You guys!" Terry's voice wailed like a saxophone, echoing against the walls.

David put his sandwich down. "Maybe everybody else is scared of you, Isaacson. But I'm not."

Their eyes were locked now. Both had put their food down. "Maybe you should be scared of me, David," Randy said quietly.

The stream chuckled. The stalactites dripped.

"Neil!" Terry shouted. "Say something to them. Make them stop."

Neil shrugged. "They're big boys. They can do what they want." His heart was beating fast.

Randy and David were still staring at each other. "Well?" Randy said. "Are you all talk or what?"

David stood. "No. I'm not."

Randy stood up and dusted imaginary crumbs off his hands. "Fine."

Neil was breathing hard. They were equally dangerous when in a rage. There was no telling what would happen now.

Like dancers, they sidestepped to a clear space away from the stream and the two other boys. This also put them out of direct light. Neil had to lean forward and squint to see them clearly. He'd never realized it before, because Randy was so dark and David was so light, but when they moved, they could be identical twins. They had the same tautness, the same feral grace.

"I want you to know something," David said to Randy. "I've never liked you one bit."

Randy's chin lifted. "I never thought about you enough to have an opinion."

On some unseen sign, they both moved. Neil caught his breath.

Then he realized Terry had jumped up and literally thrown his body between them. He took a jab in the back of the head from Randy and a sickeningly loud kidney punch from David. Terry whimpered and slid down between them like a rag doll. He opened his mouth as if he couldn't breathe, and his lungs made a rattling sound.

Neil jumped to his feet.

Randy yelled at David. "Look what you did!"

David crouched down by Terry. "Oh, god! Why did you do that? Are you okay?"

Terry used one hand to hold his injured back and made choppy gestures toward his backpack. Neil was already there, digging out the oxygen canister. It was bigger and heavier than he'd expected. He wondered how strong Terry was that he could have carried this so easily on his back.

"I know how to do it," David said, taking it from Neil and expertly fitting the breathing aparatus over Terry's face. "Oh, god, I'm sorry," he whined as Terry struggled to breathe.

The rasping gave way to deep breathing. Terry pushed the oxygen away and sat up slowly, still holding his side. "I'm all right!" he gasped. "But please, please, stop fighting! I can't stand it! Don't we have enough trouble? Do we have to have this kind of shit, too?" He shifted, twisting as if he'd felt a stab of pain.

David tried to reach for Terry. "I'm so sorry. Oh, god, I'm sorry."

Terry pushed his hands away and sat up. "It's okay, but please, David. Please. I can't stand to see people fight. I just can't stand it. All we have is each other right now . . . we . . ." He trailed off and lowered his head.

"Yes," David said. "You're right. We're sorry. I'm stupid." He cocked his head back. "Randy, I'm sorry. Really. I get . . . carried away." David stood up, pulling Terry up with him.

Randy had been sort of frozen but now he shifted his weight from one foot to the other. "Well, if we're passing out prizes for being an asshole . . ." He touched Terry lightly on the back of the head. "Did I get you bad?"

"Which one of us hurt you *more*?" David said, giving Randy a wicked grin.

"You both hit like girls." Terry shook David off and limped back to the picnic area, where Neil was still standing, feeling confused.

Terry eased himself down and picked up his sandwich. "Could we please eat?"

Randy and David shuffled over like two shamed children, resuming their places on the ground.

Neil felt guilty but kept his mouth shut. He knew

very well that he'd started this. Everyone seemed to
have forgotten that. He also wondered why he'd
wanted his best friend and his brother to hurt each
other and why the hell he felt so disappointed, now
that it hadn't happened.

SIX

Neil waited a decent interval, then went to the "bathroom" himself. Just outside The Chamber, a tunnel branched off to the right of the spring. Over the arch of rock, Randy had neatly lettered BOYS.

Neil ducked his head and went in. He swept the area with his flashlight beam and found David's shovel propped against the left wall. Near that was a patch of freshly turned earth.

I wonder if the army is like this. Neil took a minute to consider logistics. He propped his flashlight against the wall like a tiny floor lamp. That gave him a five-foot circle of very murky orange light. He dug a hole, unable to get the image of his cat, Tanner, out of his mind, then propped the shovel beside the flashlight.

He had a moment of resistance to opening his fly in such a shadowy, uncertain place, but urgency took over and he accomplished his mission with what he hoped, in the dim light, was fairly good aim. Then he filled in the hole. The whole operation was at least five minutes for something that took four seconds at home. Primitive people,

73

he thought, must have gone nuts just keeping up with their ordinary functions.

When he was done, Neil felt the urge to linger a minute and be alone. He made a careful light sweep up and down the tunnel (Mr. Snake was still on his mind), then crouched down, holding the flashlight between his palms, like an altar candle.

He thought about the bathroom at home, with its light blue tile and thick, fluffy white towels.

He thought about normal Saturdays when he and Randy might be shooting baskets out in the driveway. David, mowing the lawn, would bitch, every time he took a break, about how unfair it was and how mean they were for not letting him play.

Even though it was October, Neil made it summer in his mental picture. He closed his eyes and could smell the grass clippings and the hot blacktop—even the smell of the basketball, which was one of his favorite things. His father was out playing golf, he decided, and Tanner was rolling around under the privets, getting his fur all dusty. Mom was in the kitchen making some kind of lunch for them—sloppy joes and fresh-squeezed lemonade. Neil added the smell of onions and frying meat to his mental collage.

Then he opened his eyes and thought about what might really be going on. His mom wouldn't be worried yet. She'd just be mad because he and David had gone off for lunch somewhere and not told her. She might call Randy's or Terry's house, just to compare notes.

By two-thirty, she'd know something was wrong,

because Neil had a job at the mall from three to eight on Saturdays. She'd call there and find out he hadn't shown up for work and then she'd freak. Neil didn't ditch things. Still, she'd want to put off the idea there was a disaster. She'd work herself into a rage, telling herself they'd all gone off to the beach and lost track of time. She'd rehearse a lecture.

Dad would get home and they'd debate the whole thing. He wouldn't listen to the possibility that anything was wrong. He'd try to read the paper or something, to show he wasn't worried. Mom would be at the window by this time, trying to will the image of Neil's car over the horizon. He could see her face, the light from the window making a silvery edge on her brown hair. Her hard jawline, which Neil had inherited, would be tilted up, defying the fates. But her eyes, wide and childlike, would show how scared she really was. After a while, she'd turn to Dad in frustration and tell him that, somehow, this was all his fault.

About eight months after Mimi's funeral, David had run a traffic light with his bike, swerved to avoid an oncoming car and crashed into a utility pole. He was okay, but he came home with a dented bike and a mess of scrapes on his face and forearms. Their mother had gone ballistic on him. "What kind of idiot are you?" she had yelled.

David had taken it all with his head down. "Probably every kind there is," he'd said and slunk off to their room for the rest of the day.

That night, when they were reading in bed, their

father had come in, as he often did, to translate and apologize for their mother. David had been forgiving, simply saying, "At least she didn't belt me one."

Then their father had made a statement that had stayed with Neil ever since. He'd said, "You have to understand, son. Now that Mimi's gone, the two of you are just a little more precious."

When he'd heard those words, Neil felt his spine clench. He understood what Dad meant and it was supposed to be a loving statement, but somehow the idea had always left Neil vaguely afraid.

They'd be frantic by nightfall, all four mothers calling each other, combing their memories for clues. By late night, there would be police cars in their driveways. Randy's father would finally get involved. Everyone would turn on everyone. Crying, losing tempers. Terry's parents would be thinking about milk cartons and offering rewards. Nobody would remember to feed Tanner. Neil squeezed his eyes shut and forced out two little tears.

That's enough. He stood and went back to the main tunnel and knelt by the spring to wash his hands.

The laughter from The Chamber was echoing loudly. Neil felt left out. Maybe they were talking about him. He was about to give himself a lecture on paranoia, then remembered that they'd all talked about Randy the minute he left.

Neil washed his hands and put his face into the stream of water. He took a drink straight from the spring. It tasted faintly sulfuric, but he wasn't worried. David had had his drink a long time ago and still felt fine. The water was cool and the soft rhythm of it was soothing. He wiped his face on his shirt.

Another peal of laughter rang out. *They think I'm a joke. He tries to be Mr. Perfect, but think about it. He screws up everything he does.*

Bullshit, he argued with himself. *That's what you think of yourself. They're probably telling dirty jokes.*

All the same, Neil turned off his flashlight as he approached The Chamber and walked on the balls of his feet.

David was stretched out on his back beside the pool, arms propped under his head, telling one of his long stories. Randy and Terry were sitting almost at attention, leaning forward to listen.

"And I said to her, 'Well, you know what a lot of people do with pool tables. . . .'"

It is about sex, you big jerk. "Next!" Neil called out to announce himself.

"We thought you fell in," Randy said, scooting to make a place for Neil to sit. "Have you heard this story about Laura Wexler and the pool table?"

"Yeah," Neil said. "It's pretty good." David's sex life would have made a fabulous sitcom. He was a good storyteller, too. When they were kids, he could make up stories to tell to Mimi. Neil could only read to her.

"I'm definitely next in the bathroom," David said. "But let me finish this first. So Laura said, 'I don't know when my mom is coming home.' And I said, 'Look, let's just get up there and make out and if we hear her, we jump down and look innocent.'"

"How did you ever get a date with a girl like

Laura Wexler?" Randy asked. "That's what I want to know."

"Look at him," Neil said. "It pisses me off, too. I could have had that face. It was floating around there in the family gene pool, waiting to pop up. Instead of going to a deserving guy like me, this bad-tempered little shit gets it."

"That's why they really go for him," Randy said. "Because he's a bad-tempered little shit. Girls love that."

"If that was true," Neil said to Randy, "you'd be the one on the pool table."

"Can I finish?" David said. "So we get all the way to our underwear—"

"Did you close the curtains?" Terry interrupted.

"Grow up," David said. "Who's looking in windows that time of day? The mailman?"

"Perverts," Terry said. "They aren't like vampires. They don't wait till it's night."

"How do you know so much about perverts?" Randy asked Terry. "It sounds like you have some kind of firsthand knowledge."

"Can I tell my story?" David insisted. "I have to go to the bathroom! So anyway, we're in our underwear—"

"What does Laura Wexler look like in her underwear?" Randy asked.

David laughed. "Better than your wildest dreams, Isaacson. And everything you see is real. I checked it out thoroughly. And me and Laura were definitely cooking there. I mean, I had the feeling I was about to experience a significant event in my life, if you get what I mean."

"You're still a virgin?" Randy asked. "I thought you weren't, from the way you were talking."

"I'm getting there," David said. "I've done just about everything but. You know, fingers and mouth and—"

"Yeah," Randy said.

"And Laura could have been the one. She was having herself a good time there, hanging on to the corner pockets with both hands, calling her shots."

"The hustler meets the hustler." Neil laughed.

"And you probably didn't have any condoms with you either, did you?" Terry said.

"No, Mom, I left them in the other suit. So anyway, naturally, we hear the mother come in the front door. Adrenaline! But we're back in the family room, so I'm not going to panic. I know I have time. So we both jump down off the table and we're scrambling and—I can't find my goddamn jeans!"

Randy, the only one who had never heard this story, squeaked in surprise and then cocked his head.

"Exactly!" David said. "I couldn't figure it out either. The room is like twenty feet by fifteen feet. There's nothing there but an entertainment center, a couch and the fucking pool table. I mean, even if I, like, *threw* them off or something, they'd still be in the room somewhere!"

"Was the window open?" Randy asked.

"The window was shut." David smiled. "So now the mother is calling 'Laura! Laura!' and Laura's all dressed and she's hopping, I mean hopping up and down, whispering, 'Put on your pants!'"

Neil was laughing out loud even though he'd heard the story before.

"And I'm, like, in a cold sweat now, climbing over the couch to look behind it, and I feel like I'm in the Twilight Zone. So her mother is now in the hall, coming our way, and we don't even have the door closed—"

"Yow!" Randy said. "This is my nightmare!"

"So I do the best I can. I stay there standing behind the couch, where I'm at least partly covered. I mean, I could have tried to get down and hide, but then if she saw me, it would be worse. I don't know. Anyway, she walks in and what is she holding in her hand?"

"I hope it's not a twelve-gauge shotgun," Randy said.

"It's my jeans. My Levi's 505 jeans. In her hand."

"What?" Randy cried.

"And she says to me, 'I suppose these belong to you.' I really thought I was going to die. I could feel how red my face was."

"But how . . ." Randy said.

David smiled. "Laura's fucking German shepherd. Brandy. That fucking sneaky spy dog came in there and took the evidence and was waiting at the door for Laura's mom. It's no wonder they call them police dogs."

Randy was wiping tears as he laughed. "Oh shit!"

"So, I'm still a virgin," David concluded. "And now I really have to go to the bathroom." He stood.

"And where are you now with Laura?" Randy asked.

"I'm nowhere with Laura." David sighed. "She joins a long list of women and girls who get together and talk about what a shit I am."

"The rest of us would kill for that honor," Neil told him.

"You can have it," David said over his shoulder as he left.

Randy immediately turned to Terry. He loved to interview people, and David had obviously whetted his appetite. "So how about you?" he asked. "You break any hearts lately?"

Terry laughed politely. Randy waited expectantly. Silence. In a second it was a contest. They gazed opaquely at each other. Randy's look became a demand. Terry's look, a polite but firm refusal. Neil was kind of impressed. He hadn't known Terry could hold his ground like that.

"Okay." Randy said finally. He swiveled to Neil. "Let's turn the camera on you. Is it my imagination or have you been sort of out of service lately?"

Neil turned to Terry, looking for an ally. "This is how he avoids talking about himself. Randy's about to join a twelve-step program for bimbo-holics."

"Excuse me?" Randy said. "Who's trying not to talk about himself? I know I have a bimbo problem. I've got a bimbo monkey on my back. I'm comfortable with that. So back to you, Neil. You broke up with Ann Schulteiss three months ago and since then, it's all quiet on the western front. So what's going on?"

Neil felt almost panicky. David came back and sat

down and joined the other two in staring at him, even though he didn't know what the question was. "Do you really want to know?" Neil said finally.

"God!" said Randy. "Maybe I don't! Are you into something weird?"

The younger boys swung their gaze from Randy to Neil.

"No!" Neil said, activating the echo. "I mean . . . I was going to tell you. . . . I don't think now is exactly the best time . . . but . . . I was kind of thinking about asking . . . Chloe out."

Randy didn't move a muscle. Yet somehow his whole expression changed. "Chloe who?"

Neil looked down at the dirt. "Chloe Isaacson. Your sister."

"Wow!" Terry said, like a viewer responding to an interesting TV program.

"Chloe, my . . . sister," Randy clarified. He raised two fingers to his chest and thumped his heart. "My sister Chloe."

"Yes!" Neil yelled. "Is that so crazy?"

"How long has *this* been going on?" Randy demanded.

Neil felt a sweat break out all over his body. "There's nothing going on! You asked me who I like, that's all! I knew you wouldn't be crazy about this—"

"How do you know anything!" Randy shot back. He leaned in toward Neil and shouted into his face. "What do you mean, you knew! I don't even know how I feel yet! You know why? Because I never know what's going on with you! You know why? Because you don't fucking tell me! You know why? Because you think it's fine to hear every nasty little detail of what's going on with me but you don't want me to have a clue what's going on with you! I guess you're just Jesus Christ back on Earth and you don't need any friends because you're happy keeping your little secrets! So now you're going behind my back in my own house with my own sister and I still have to read about it in the papers with everybody else! If I wasn't stuck in here with you, I'd be gone by now. I'd hitchhike home. I'd get as far away from your smug face as I could, because I'm so sick of your superior shit I could puke! I don't even care anymore, Neil. How's that? I don't even care what's up with you. Date my mom. Date my dad. Date my fucking dog! I just don't care!"

Everyone sat very still while Randy's multiple echoes died away. His voice seemed to be everywhere. It reminded Neil of the bats. *I feel okay,* Neil said to himself. *I'm not upset. Randy's just like this. I knew he'd hate the idea and I was right. The mistake I made was telling him.*

"Join the club, Randy," David said into the silence. "Are you just finding all this stuff out about him?"

Neil looked up and locked eyes with his brother. "Thanks," he said. "Were you afraid he didn't cut me up enough? Did you want to do the coup de grace?"

"Why are you guys doing this?" Terry said. Instead of the usual wail, his voice was low and calm. It sounded as if an adult had just spoken in a roomful of children. Neil looked at him. Terry was sitting with his knees pulled up, rocking himself, his face pale. He still looked like a little kid. But that voice came from somewhere else. "Is this what tough guys like you do when you're scared? You shit on each other and then you feel better? Because I really don't get it. We're trapped in here. We're lost. We might never get home. . . ." His voice broke. He paused and went on. "So why isn't that the important thing right now? I mean, what is the difference whether Neil likes Chloe or if he keeps secrets? Why should we give a rat's ass? Maybe none of us will ever go on a date again. How's that? If you want something to get upset about, how's that?"

No one answered him. They shot guilty looks at each other.

David looked at his watch. "We do have more important things to do, and it's getting late. It's two o'clock."

Neil kept his eyes down. "Randy, I'm sorry," he muttered.

Randy sighed. "Me, too. Now I've shit on two people. I'm doing good today." He turned to Terry. "You want to be next?"

"Don't even try." Terry grinned. "I'm the one who's on to you, remember?"

David started picking up the lunch trash, folding all the plastic neatly and putting it away in his backpack. "I, for one, don't like the feeling that Terry is coming off mature here. It's unnatural. Neil, I'm sorry, too. I just took a kick because you were down."

Neil still felt immobilized. It always took him too long to get over things. His body felt as if it had been run over by trucks. "No problem," he lied. He faked a laugh. "Maybe it's good we're all splitting up for a while."

Everyone exchanged glances. It didn't look as if anyone was happy about that.

"Well?" David said. "What are we waiting for?"

Randy stood first. "I'm waiting for my alarm clock to ring and my mom to tell me I'm going to be late for school." He paused, as if actually expecting to wake up. "Oh well," he said. He shouldered his pack, picked up his Betadine and flicked on his flashlight. Slowly the others followed.

SEVEN

Mimi had been different from Neil and David. Freer. Happier. Things that went through her head popped right out of her mouth. If she didn't like how they sounded, she just rolled her eyes and said, "Whoops! I didn't mean that!"

So different from David, for instance, who tortured his thoughts to death and announced all his important statements with long preambles. Or Neil, who left most of his serious thoughts and feelings unsaid.

Neil didn't know why he was thinking so much about Mimi now. Was it being underground? The darkness? The feeling of graves?

Maybe, Neil thought, it was because they were all going to die.

After lunch, the boys had walked out of The Chamber together, into the spring tunnel, past the boys' room. As forks and side tunnels presented themselves, the group had splintered. Randy was first, off to the left, all of them watching the darkness slowly swallow his light. Then David had chosen a tunnel and ducked away suddenly. Neil and Terry had walked together in si-

86

lence, passing up several opportunities to separate, postponing the moment they would each have to be alone.

Finally, at a large tunnel, Terry cleared his throat and said, "All right!" And he took the plunge. Neil had stopped walking and watched Terry's light, which was bouncy like his walk, until he couldn't tell whether he was seeing it or imagining it.

That leaves me as the biggest coward. Neil forced himself to take the very next tunnel—a bad tunnel, he now felt, too cramped, too cold, the stone walls sharp and hostile.

Every ten yards or so he wrote NG in Betadine on the wall. The chemical smelled terrible, like a veterinarian's office. The smell seemed to fill the little tunnel. Once, when Neil had turned his light up to the wall to write, something had scuttled away, making a sound like dry paper. He had scanned frantically up and down the wall, trying to find it just so he could know what it was. Palmetto? Scorpion? Troll? Whatever it was, it was too quick or too good at finding crevices. When he walked on from that spot, his legs shook.

With each step, Neil had developed the habit of sweeping his light from left to right across the cave floor, systematically checking for rattlesnakes or anything else he didn't want to step on.

His claustrophobia was back, now that he was alone in a smaller tunnel again. In the big chamber it had seemed all right. But now he was alert again for any narrowing or signs of a ceiling caving in. It was a nagging, annoying kind of feeling, like when you're reading a book and, on some dim level, you know there's a fly in the room.

Mostly Neil was angry with himself for choosing this moment in his life to think about Mimi. *I haven't got enough trouble with the present? I have to go back to the worst time in my life and add that?*

He remembered how he and David used to take her to the park. They had a little game they played crossing streets, so Mimi would hold their hands. They would count one-two-three and swing her up over the curbs. No matter how many times they did it, Mimi would always shriek with excitement, as if she were terrified they were going to drop her. They never did.

The shakes in Neil's knees suddenly got worse and he fell. *You jerk!* He forced himself to stand. "You big jerk!" he said out loud. He'd been watching horror movies all his life and he knew one thing for sure. Brave people survive. Scared people die.

He and David had a passion for slice-and-dice movies. They loved to size up the whole cast of characters in the first ten minutes and decide what order the filmmaker would have them die in. First in line were minorities. Then nerds and class-clown types. That left a group of about ten attractive WASPS for the main body of the film. Then they were eliminated by character traits. About half an hour into the film, the oversexed couple would get it, usually while they were in the act. After that, the cowards. Then anyone who was mean or cruel. The last ones to go were the unbelievers, the ones who said there was a rational explanation for the whole thing. They always died a horrible death. Finally you'd be left with either a couple or a girl alone. The survivors were always virgins and they were resourceful, smart, tough and brave. *No one like that in this group,* Neil thought sadly.

Neil noticed he was sweating in odd places. His body was just getting fabulously creative in its different ways of telling him he was scared. He figured the temperature in his tunnel was about sixty degrees and here he was with sweat pouring off him. He wondered whether he should or shouldn't drink water. Then the shakes started again. Along with a nice, ice pick–through–the–temple headache.

All right. Enough of trying to go without a fix.

He sat down and took out his Baudelaire. It was an oversize paperback edition, the pages frayed from heavy use. Neil held it between his hands. Instantly he felt calmer.

It was funny, how the whole Baudelaire thing had happened. How it rescued Neil after the funeral. He had never been a poetry reader. Still wasn't. But his mom was. She'd been an English major in college and kept shelves and shelves of poetry anthologies in the den. She was a Blake fan, saw things in Blake she couldn't get anyone else in the family to appreciate. Neil and David used Blake for their private jokes. *Look out! Here comes the invisible worm that flies in the night!* Mom had sighed and given up on having literary sons.

The day of the funeral, the early part at least, was weird in Neil's mind. For one thing, the whole family was staying at a Holiday Inn because the house had just burned down. Going to a cemetery from a Holiday Inn was very weird. And at that point in time, just the fact of Mimi being dead was still an impossible thing. You can't go to your job at the mall one day and get a call saying, "Come home, your house burned down and your sister is dead." Your brain just says no. It says, *No, a minute ago I was wondering if I could afford to go to the food court on my break and get a Coke.* Five minutes later you can't be told your sister and your house are gone.

So you go home and your house *is* gone and rescue vehicles and news trucks are all over the neighborhood and your mother and father are talking gibberish and they tell you your brother is in a hospital somewhere for smoke inhalation and your sister is in a different hospital, even though she's already dead. And if you want to, you can walk through the smoldering pile of junk and look for your melted sports trophies or your pictures of yourself in the first grade. You don't want to. You just turn your back and look at the houses across the street and *hate* those people who still have everything.

And while you're seeing your cat across the street under a hedge and crying with relief that at least *he's* not dead, your father is trying to tell you this crazy story about your brother, who wouldn't sip a beer on a dare, smoking pot and getting stoned and causing all this destruction. And you think about how innocently you bought this little joint to hide in your room, just to try one time, so you wouldn't feel like such a straight arrow with your friends. You could say, when the topic came up, I tried it, I didn't like it. Only you didn't get to try it, because apparently your little brother found it and even though he won't drink iced tea because of the caffeine, somehow he decided to go wild that day and he got mellow and let the thing burn and it set fire to the whole house. And your father says he found your brother facedown on the lawn with little holes in his clothes from where sparks were showering down on him. And your father says your sister's room was situated so that she couldn't get out past the fire in the hall and her window, which was old and jammed shut, wouldn't open for her and you start screaming in your mind, MIMI, WHY DIDN'T YOU THINK TO BREAK IT? YOU'RE A SMART KID! YOU WOULD THINK OF BREAKING THE WINDOW! DID YOU THINK YOU'D GET IN TROUBLE?

Then you're supposed to go to a Holiday Inn like it was a vacation or something. And your brother is let out of the hospital but no one touches him or speaks to him, as if part of him is still on fire. And they make you go shopping for something to wear to the funeral because you don't have clothes anymore. You don't have anything. And you're in a room in a hotel with your brother and he can't talk and you can't talk and nobody talks before the funeral and your mother keeps going back to that pile of junk and looking for stuff she can save and your parents' room at the Holiday Inn is filling up with charred, wet, smelly junk she thinks will be useful when you start over. Start over. And mostly what she seems to be collecting are her poetry books, even though the pages are stuck together and they smell like a pile of dead bats. Like she thinks maybe the poetry inside will heal them.

And after the funeral, you have this realization that

you've been gone for about four days and you haven't said anything. Not "Pass the salt," not "Mimi, come back," not anything. And no one seems to have noticed.

And one morning, you leave your room because you have to get away from your brother for a while and you stand by this sparkling deserted Holiday Inn pool and you think you'd better say something out loud just so you know you can do it. And you really plan to speak but you don't and you think, *I guess this is what going crazy feels like*.

And the sparkling water starts to hurt your eyes and you have a headache and it really pisses you off that the pool is so cheerful, like it's making fun of you somehow.

So you leave but you don't want to go back to your room because your brother's there and so you go to your parents' room because they went off to talk to lawyers or insurance people or something. You feel dirty, sneaky, going into their room, but then even that feeling doesn't last and you just go back to blankness.

And in there is that pile of charred, nasty books along with some pots and pans and handbags and things she's saved. And you're even worse off than you knew because suddenly your knees give way and you knock over the pile of books and you aren't even crying, you aren't even screaming, just getting more and more silent inside. You're lying on the carpet and you think, *Somebody help me, somebody find me!* And you grab one of the books in the pile, hoping it will save you somehow. You wonder if you can even read

92

as you scrabble through the pages. First all the letters and symbols are a blur, but then you can read, you can read. And this is what you find:

Soon we shall plunge into the shadows cold;
Farewell, the brilliance of brief summers gone!
Already I can hear the sad trees felled,
The wood resounding on the courtyard stone.

All winter will return into my soul:
Hate, anger, horror, toil, and sudden chill,
And, like the sun in its antarctic hell,
My heart, a red and frozen block, is still.

I listen, trembling, to each log that falls;
The scaffold being built echoes less dull.
My spirit broken like a citadel
By heavy battering-rams infallible.

I feel, lulled by these blows monotonous,
As if, quickly, a coffin were nailed down.
For whom?—Summer is dead; here autumn is!
This strange sound echoes as for someone gone.

Everything inside you explodes at once and you find yourself on the pretty blue Holiday Inn carpet, crying so hard your nose is running, and clutching this book with white knuckles and you hear yourself wail. You roll around on the pretty blue carpet and maybe all the tears you've stored up all your life come out in that one explosion because now you know that someone, somewhere (you can't read his name for the tears in your eyes), but someone, felt just like you do right now.

And you steal this book from your mother and when it falls apart you go out and buy a new edition and you look up the guy and even though you find out he was one of the biggest losers the earth has ever known and not the kind of person you'd pick for a hero, you still love his poems, all of them, and you read the poems when you can't sleep or can't talk or can't cry. Because he knows you. He's the only person you've ever found who knows you.

3:30 P.M., SATURDAY

Baudelaire had been the perfect poet for grief. However, Neil realized, he was not so hot when a guy was working on the will to survive.

Neil had wedged himself like a cockroach into a little alcove of stone. His knees were pulled up, with the flashlight tucked between them to make a reading light. His fingers restlessly flipped the pages, looking for one of those passages that used to loosen the tightly packed pain inside him. But something had gone wrong.

— O sorrow! sorrow! Time eats life away,
The Foe obscure which does our hearts consume
grows stronger on the blood of our decay!

"Fuck you!" Neil said out loud to Baudelaire. "To each his own, Charlie, but right at the moment, you're really pissing me off." He continued to talk out loud because it felt good. "I think personally," he explained, unzipping his backpack, "that there's a time to lie down and cry and there's a time to get up and strap your balls on and get moving." He slid the book into the pack

95

and gave it a gentle pat, as if it were a dog he was commanding to stay. He slung the pack over his shoulder, working the Betadine bottle out of his jeans pocket as he stood. "It's not like I'm not grateful to you and everything," he said. "I mean you were really good for me when Mimi died. You sort of helped me . . . collapse. But I can't collapse now. I've got these guys in here with me and I've got to get them out."

He began to walk, flashlight sweeping the ground in rhythmic arcs. Neil was tired of talking to Baudelaire, but he liked the feeling of talking, so he switched gears. "So, Mom," he said. "I guess I screwed up and brought the wrong poet in here with me. You would have known what to do." He stopped and printed his initials on the wall. "This is why we have to ask our parents' permission for things. Mom would have said, 'Neil, you asshole. Don't take your Baudelaire. You need some Kipling or Robert Bly if you're going in a cave. What's wrong with you, boy?'" He giggled, but didn't care for the loose, sloppy sound of the giggle echoing back.

"You know," he said, not sure who he was talking to now. "It might be kind of a bad sign, a guy starting to talk to his mother and make up answers for her." He paused and marked the wall again. The G came out illegible and he had to do it again. Then he thought how stupid it was to worry about neatness at a time like this. Then he thought he'd be embarrassed if Randy or someone came along this way and saw he'd been stupid enough to worry about how legible his printing was. Then he thought everything he'd just been thinking sounded crazy.

"I think I'd know if I were going crazy," he said. "If I were going crazy, I'd be *talking* to myself or something!" He laughed, but it felt more like some kind of muscle spasm. The last time he'd caught himself laughing like that was when the rattlesnake was about to bite him.

"What is it with you, Neil?" he asked himself. "Doom cracks you up? Being in danger is a source of amusement? I really don't think this situation is funny at all!"

He decided to stop talking for a while. He looked at his watch. It was 3:30 P.M. "You'd better hurry up and find the way out, Neil," he said. "It's getting late in the day." Then he remembered he'd decided not to talk out loud anymore. "Shut up!" he said.

He stopped to print his initials. They came out backwards, GN instead of NG. "So what?" he said and then realized he was *still* talking. He started walking a little faster so he wouldn't think so much.

He'd always felt that his mind was too active for its own good. He'd seen David, sometimes, staring into space like an Indian. David could turn into stone anytime he wanted to. Neil would ask, "What are you thinking about?" David would say, "Nothing." And Neil believed him. He envied it.

"I'll decide *what* I want to think about," Neil said. "That way I get control of it. What would be the right thing to think about now?"

Suddenly he stumbled, tripping on a vein of rock that ran through the dirt floor. Adrenaline shot through him and sweat broke out on his face. "Don't think about *that*," he said.

He placed his initials slowly and carefully on the wall. Then he walked on, pacing his steps and breathing a little slower, a little more deliberate.

This is like basketball, he thought. *I need to visualize success. I need to put my feelings on hold and be goal driven. So here's what I'll think about. There's a way out of this cave and I will walk until I find it. There's a way out of this cave and I will walk until I find it.* He came to a fork and confidently chose the left, feeling guided. *There's a way out of this cave and I will walk until I find it.* Another fork. One of the tunnels looked a little lighter than the other. Neil chose that one, feeling a surge of confidence, joy almost. *There's a way out of this cave and I will walk until I find it. There's a way out of this cave—time to write my initials again—and I'll walk. . . .* As Neil turned his light to the wall, he saw something marked on the wall a few feet ahead. Something the color of Betadine.

On the wall *ahead* of him.

"There's a way," he said softly. His marking hand fell limp at his side. Slowly, he walked toward the other marking. He knew what he was going to see. His chest felt heavy.

"There's a way," he said brokenly. "There's a way out. . . ." He stood in front of the marking, his light shining on it. His own initials, nice and neat, put there an hour ago. In the distance he heard the rush of water, laughing at him.

Something hot and horrible, like a storm of blood, roared up through his body. "NO!" he screamed. "GOD DAMN IT! NO!"

His right arm, with a will of its own, hurled the Betadine bottle at the rock wall. It bounced on the rocks and came open, filling the air with nose-burning chemicals. Brown fluid oozed down the wall, like blood.

Not enough. He threw himself at the rocks, dropping his flashlight, letting the darkness swallow him. His arm swung up and pounded the wall. SLAM! SLAM! SLAM!

The pain made him even madder. He would kill this cave! It was trying to kill him and he wanted out! He wanted out right now! SLAM! SLAM! SLAM! He drove his knee into the rock as if it were a stubborn door.

He heard a voice, high and screaming, as his other fist came up and beat the stone, too. *That's me screaming. I'm screaming.*

———

The rocks under his right fist were slippery now, wet with blood, but Neil didn't care. He would fight this cave to the death.

His arms ached. He wondered if any of his fingers were broken. His screaming was getting hoarse and he knew that in a minute he was going to pass out, which was fine, because what did it matter? He was dead, anyway.

As his voice frayed out and his blows to the wall came heavier and slower, he heard something new in the distance. Footsteps running up behind him.

He stopped hitting the wall and slid down, right

hand dragging in the blood, sore knee buckling and making him fall awkwardly on his side. "Help," he called to whoever it was. "Help me."

"Oh, god, Neil, what happened to you? What are you doing?"

Terry's voice. Confused and weary, Neil also felt relieved. Better to be a coward in front of another coward. His body twisted from the wall to face the light. Terry's approaching light blinded him. "I'm okay," Neil said in an old man's voice. He put his right arm up to fight the glare and found that it was dripping with blood. He had scraped off the skin on one whole side of his hand. Trying to beat up a cave.

Terry hopped around the disaster site like a bird, setting his own flashlight upright like a lamp, finding Neil's and doing the same with it. "Oh shit!" he said, when he could see clearly. "Neil, you're bleeding! You've got—why is your *hand* bleeding like that?" He stripped off his yellow polo shirt. Neil was surprised to see he had hair on his chest.

"I don't know," Neil said. "I got bored and started injuring myself for fun."

Terry ripped open a seam in his shirt. He paused and blinked at Neil. "Don't play like you're going crazy if you're not. This is scary enough."

"I'm sorry," Neil said.

"Are you hurt anyplace else?" Terry asked. He took Neil's right hand and began to stroke Betadine on it.

"Shit!" Neil flinched, feeling the burn all the way up his arm.

"Sorry." Terry took the piece of shirt he'd carefully torn and wrapped it around Neil's hand several times,

100

tucking in the ends. It looked as if he knew what he was doing. "Neil, it looked like you were kind of, throwing your whole body at the rocks. We need to see if you hurt yourself anyplace else. Why didn't we think to split up the stuff in the first aid kit!"

Neil sighed like a weary child. "My left knee is hurt. I rammed it into the wall."

Terry was blushing so hard it was visible, even by flashlight. "Well, we should disinfect that, too. I'll do it or you can—"

"I can do it," Neil said. He took the Betadine bottle and shoved his jeans down to his ankles. His knee and shin were red and scraped, would be a mass of bruises by tomorrow. He delicately touched the knee-cap, trying to figure out what a break would feel like. He decided that was too terrible to consider. He stroked the scraped skin with Betadine, wincing from the pain.

"What happened?" Terry asked.

Neil looked up and saw that Terry was standing with his arms around his stomach, staring intently away. This kid had a real thing about modesty!

"I went crazy is what happened," Neil said, giving the wounds a second coat. "I found out I had made a circle. I came back on my own initials—ow!—and I just went nuts and threw my stuff against the wall and then I started hitting the wall, I guess, and that's how I hurt my hand." Neil finished quickly, anxious to get dressed again. Terry's excessive shyness was rubbing off on him.

Terry shuddered. "You guys are all so angry."

Neil pulled up his jeans, noticing that Terry's ban-

101

dage was working beautifully, staying nice and tight but not cutting off circulation. Neil knew he couldn't have done as well, and he'd grown up with medical emergencies, having a doctor for a father. "Aren't *you* angry?" Neil replied. "Doesn't it make you mad that we're stuck in here and can't get out?" Neil pulled up his zipper.

Obviously responding to that all-clear signal, Terry let go of his stomach and looked at Neil again. "No! I'm scared. I mean, getting mad seems a little stupid, doesn't it? It's not like the cave is doing this to us on purpose." Terry sat on the ground opposite Neil and unzipped his pack. "Want a cookie?"

Neil laughed. "What about the rationing committee? Don't we have to file a petition in triplicate to get a cookie?"

Terry smiled. "Not if the committee isn't here."

"Wait," Neil said. "Would you rather have one of my candy bars? I've got two. It works out perfectly."

Terry's smile grew. He was actually kind of a handsome kid. "I never turn down chocolate!"

Savoring the chocolate and drinking cold spring water from the canteen, Neil felt almost human again. Even the sting of the Betadine burning into his cuts was strangely comforting. "I've been through more feelings in this one day than the whole rest of my life," he said to Terry. "I really think I'm losing it. Like right now I feel good. Maybe it's the sugar or something."

Terry had leaned back and propped one arm under his head to eat the candy bar. Now that he was shirtless and displaying all this body hair, it was impossible to see him as a little boy anymore. "It's not that. It's because a while back you were feeling so bad. It's like you get a . . . bounce . . . when something really bad is over. Like when my parents have a fight? The next day, I'll be walking around like a jerk, looking at how pretty the sky is and everything."

"How bad are those fights?" Neil asked carefully. He and Terry had never talked about personal things before.

Terry took a big bite of chocolate. "Bad."

"Does your dad . . . beat your mom?" Neil didn't know why he asked, but he already knew the answer. There was something about Mrs. Quinn, the way she drifted around the house like smoke, trying to be invisible. The way she smiled all the time, even when her eyes were tired or angry or sad.

Terry looked at Neil a long time before answering. "Yes."

"Does he ever beat you?" Neil knew this, too, without being told. Even though Mr. Quinn had always been pleasant and hearty when he and David had been over there. There was something . . . A picture flashed in his mind of Mr. Quinn reaching behind Terry once to get the remote control. Terry had jumped a mile, just from seeing his father's arm move in his direction.

Terry was staring into his candy bar, pretending to study the layers. "I guess David's been telling stories."

"No! No, I swear. I just knew. I can't explain. Sometimes you just know things."

"Mostly he picks on her," Terry said quietly. "But sometimes I get in the middle of it and he goes for me instead."

"How nice," Neil said.

"Did David tell you I was adopted?" Terry lifted his eyes to Neil's with something like triumph.

"No! Are you kidding?"

"Nope. They couldn't have a kid. They adopted me when I was two. Sometimes I'm really glad. I mean, he's such a jerk and she . . . I'm just glad I'm not really connected to them. That sounds horrible, I bet."

"It sounds okay to me."

They finished their candy in silence.

"You've got your shit, too," Terry said, after a while. "Mimi and all that."

Neil slumped. "Yeah. All that."

Terry looked at Neil cautiously. "Randy doesn't know?"

Neil forced himself to sit up straight. "I'm not into that, Terry. I don't think you have to tell all your private crap to your friends. Nobody really wants to hear it anyway."

Terry laughed. "So if you think people aren't interested in other people's crap, why'd you ask me all those questions?"

Neil laughed. "I don't know, Sherlock. Why did I?"

Terry shrugged. "I figured it was because you cared."

"It was."

Terry crumpled his candy paper into a ball, rolling it back and forth between his palms. "So why do you go around acting like nobody should care about you?" Terry's dark eyes were calm and steady. Gentle, but somehow defiant. Neil realized he'd known this kid all his life and never understood him.

"Eat shit and die," Neil said mildly.

Terry laughed. "Can I have a drink of water?"

Neil passed the canteen. "You want to hear something personal? Is that the little slumber party game we're playing here? Okay. Here's something personal. I've got claustrophobia, Terry. Now take a minute to realize how funny that is. We're stuck in a cave and I've got claustrophobia. I've been batshit nuts since ten this morning. Back when you guys were still having fun, I was already unraveling like a bad sock. And now—I won't even tell you how bad off I am right now."

Terry was giggling. His laughter echoed into the canteen he held to his mouth. "Neil, news flash. You gave some of this away when you started boxing with the walls. Sorry to disappoint you."

Neil felt very lonely. "You don't understand, Terry. I can't stand to be weak." His voice went hoarse on the last word, illustrating its meaning.

None of this seemed to be shocking or upsetting to Terry. "I know. David's the same way. Randy's the same way. Probably all normal guys are. There's probably something wrong with me since I'm not killing snakes and picking fights and smashing things."

"I bet you'll last the longest," Neil said. "You're sitting there looking perfectly calm and I'm bleeding in two places."

"I'm not calm." Terry took a long drink and wiped

his mouth. "Trust me." He handed the canteen back to Neil.

There was a brief silence.

"Don't tell anybody," Neil said. "What I said to you or what you saw me do."

"I knew *that* was coming!"

"I mean it. I don't want those other guys knowing what a wimp I am. Please."

"Why would I tell them?"

"Just promise you won't. Okay?"

"I promise. Promise you won't feel sorry for me for having such bad parents."

"It's a deal."

"I wonder what time it is," Terry said.

Neil didn't want to know. "It's late."

Terry adopted a spooky voice. "It's later than we think," he intoned.

"Where did you come from, anyway?" Neil asked.

"How do I know? We're lost! I just heard you screaming and followed the sound."

"Have you been walking all that time? Steadily? Since lunch?"

"Yes."

Neil closed his eyes. "That means your tunnel of choice made a circle just like mine. Can you hear the water? We're like ten yards from the place we ate lunch!"

"Good," Terry said. "When everybody else shows up, we can have dinner."

"It's not funny," Neil said.

"One of us has to look at their watch, Neil."

"Let's look together." Neil looked. It was four-thirty. "Shit!"

Terry reached for his pack. "So we should—"

"No! We can't give up yet. Let's try one more tunnel. Together."

"We'd have to go together. You smashed your trail-marking kit. But I don't think we should go against the plan. The one important thing when you're separated from people is to be where you said you'd be when you said you'd be there. Otherwise, everybody goes looking for everybody else and you might never get together."

"What? Did you write a book on this or something?"

Terry grinned. "My mom used to lose me in department stores."

Neil grinned back. "But you were too smart for her, weren't you, kid?"

"You know it."

They stood up together. Terry started back but Neil hesitated. "I hate to give up like this!"

Terry sighed. "I can see that. Just let me be in charge here. I'm an expert in giving up and slinking off in defeat."

Neil laughed. "I see why my brother likes you."

"Thanks."

They fell into step, following the sound of water. "David likes you, too, you know," Terry said, glancing sideways at Neil.

Instantly Neil felt angry. "Well, of course he does. We're brothers and all. You know?"

"He looks up to you."

Neil realized he'd been holding his breath and let it out. "What's your *point*, Terry?"

"Nothing," Terry said quickly. "It's none of my business."

"Got that right."

They finished their walk in silence, the sound of the spring growing louder and louder, like mocking applause.

5:00 P.M., SATURDAY

The main chamber glowed with a dense peach-colored light in the late afternoon. David was already there, kneeling by the pool, filling his canteen. His cap was off and his head was bent, so his brassy hair spilled forward, catching the light and making him the brightest thing in the murky room.

Neil trudged in beside Terry, feeling heavy and defeated. Still, he was happy about seeing this chamber again; the calcite formations like huge piles of melted ice cream, the crystals sparkling in the ceiling, the stream rushing into the still pool. In a strange way, this part of the cave felt like home. It was cooler here, too. The air smelled fresh and watery.

David looked up, apparently hearing their footsteps. He had to be part Indian, Neil thought. His eyes widened. "What happened to you?" He jumped up and rushed toward Neil, then stopped short and looked at Terry. "Where's your shirt?"

Neil found himself backing up. "It's nothing," he snapped. He put his hand behind his back as David reached for it.

109

"He fell and scraped his knee and got a bad scrape on his hand," Terry said. "It really knocked the skin off. I had to use my shirt to—"

"How bad is it?" David said. "Let me see it!" He turned to Terry. "Did you wash it before you wrapped it up like that?"

"I put Betadine on it," Terry said. "You can see it under the—"

"But did you make sure and get any dirt out of there? Or little pebbles or—"

"I'm all *right*!" Neil walked away from them toward the pool. "Jesus!"

"I took the Red Cross first aid class the same time you did," Terry said. "I think I know how to bandage up a cut."

David turned to Neil. "Do you feel all right? Not feverish or—"

"If I hear one more word from either of you two old ladies, I'm going to scream!" Neil held out both hands, like a shield. "I'm fine! I fell! I'm stupid! I picked a tunnel that went in a circle and came right back here! My whole life is a fraud! There's no meaning to existence! Okay? Now we've worried about everything, David. Now you can relax."

David and Terry exchanged looks. "He's feeling a little cranky," Terry explained.

Neil sighed and turned his back on them. He felt much better now that he'd yelled at David. He watched the stream run into the pool, counting the little bubbles that rose to the agitated surface, each one dancing for a few seconds before it popped. Some bubbles were hardy and bobbed all around the pool, avoiding the extreme pressure that would shatter them. Other bubbles were crushed almost the moment they were born. There were some tiny, stubborn bubbles, like those in champagne, that tried to rush headlong into the oncoming stream. They were plowed down quickly. The big fat lazy bubbles were the survivors. The ones that went with the current.

Neil tipped his head back and looked at the sky over the ceiling fissure. It was hazy, cloudless, blue-jay blue. The bats had not returned. Sunlight struck the edges of the ceiling crystals, tipping them with flame.

"I'm worried about Randy," David was saying. "He's a half hour late."

"Randy's always a half hour late," Neil called without looking around. He felt almost cheerful again. Maybe he was still on his "bounce." Or maybe blowing out his emotional jets had been good in some way. He was also kind of stunned to realize that Terry had seen him in that pathetic state and was still treating him like a normal person. Neil had always believed if people knew what his real thoughts and feelings were like, they'd run for the hills.

David and Terry walked up behind Neil and sat down, flanking him. "You better put on my jacket," David said to Terry. "You're going to freeze to death in here without a shirt. Especially . . . tonight."

All three exchanged looks. Even though they knew that coming back here meant they had given up for the night, hearing it said was jarring.

David looked down, as if he'd said something

dirty. He unzipped his pack and pulled out his diving team jacket, tossing it over Neil's head to Terry.

"Now we don't have a tablecloth anymore," Terry complained. He put the jacket on and zipped it up.

David looked at his watch. "It's after five o'clock, Neil. What time can I start worrying about Randy?"

"Pretty soon," Neil pulled his knees up. "What if his watch broke?"

"He'd still have some sense of time," David looked toward the entrance to The Chamber. "If it was me, I'd probably come back early to make sure I didn't mess up."

"Randy's not like that," Neil looked at the entrance, too. It was very empty. "Maybe someone should go—"

"No!" Terry touched Neil's shoulder. "I'm telling you. That's the worst thing. If you go out, then you get lost and we wonder about you. Then somebody else goes out looking for you and—"

Neil turned to Terry. "Yeah, but what if he got hurt? I got hurt. We have to say, if Randy isn't back by blank o'clock, somebody goes looking for him. He left a trail. It's not like we'd be wandering around blind."

"Seven?" David said, still staring at the doorway where Randy wasn't. "No matter how loose he is about the rules, he'd definitely be back here by seven."

"Six," Neil said. "He'll come back out of hunger by six. And I can't stand to wait two hours not knowing what's going on. I mean, what if he ran into another snake or something? He might be out there right now needing help."

Terry stood. "The next time we explore a cave, I'm bringing cell phones and beepers. Excuse me, I have to go to the shovel room."

"Be back in five minutes or David will come looking for you!" Neil called after him. He turned back to David and found himself on the receiving end of a very piercing aquamarine stare.

"What really happened to your hand?" David asked.

Neil's heart skittered. "Huh?"

"What did you do? You didn't go nuts and hit Terry, did you?"

"Of course not! What do you—"

"I bet you hit a wall!"

"You're lucky my right hand is out of service, buddy, because—"

"Neil." David placed his palm on the ground between them. "I know you're not holding up so good and I—"

Neil leaned away from him. "You have gone stark, staring mad, boy! What are you talking about? Maybe you're the one going nuts. Maybe you're having hallucinations. How many fingers am I holding up?" He displayed his middle finger.

"Okay, fine," David said. "I was just trying to help—"

"I don't need your help."

"I can see that."

"Good."

"Good."

"Good."

They both turned back toward the pool. The sunlight was now bouncing off the ceiling crystals and making little confetti sparkles in the water. Neil stared at it until it was all a dancing blur, blotting out everything except the sound of David next to him, heaving a huge sigh.

Terry came back from the boys' room. "Are we meditating?" he asked, sitting down between the brothers.

David played with his cap, twirling it listlessly on one hand. "We're sick of each other and we don't feel like talking."

The light inside The Chamber was orange now. The sparkles on the water deepened to a fiery gold. Neil noticed his hand was stinging under the bandage.

"Should we eat?" Terry asked quietly.

"Not without Randy," Neil said.

Terry dug a pebble from the dirt and lobbed it into the pool. The light squiggles writhed.

Neil glared at him. "Quit it."

David grabbed Neil's arm roughly. "Don't tell him what to do!"

Neil whirled on him, ready to strike, but then saw Randy ambling through the doorway, smiling crookedly. "I guess I must be missing Happy Hour!"

Neil jumped to his feet. "You're okay!" His voice echoed loudly. Then he saw the look on Randy's face. It was a look he knew well: jaw set, eyes moving restlessly.

"Yeah, I'm doing great!" Randy strolled toward them like a killer who knows that his victims can't escape. "I'm stuck in a cave with no way out and three stupid guys who probably really smell by now and we only have enough food for twenty-four hours and nobody outside has any idea how to find us. I'm a lucky, lucky guy!" He walked around to the far side of the pool, let his pack drop to the ground and plunked himself down beside it.

Both the younger boys looked at Neil, obviously expecting him to fix this new problem. "Tomorrow will be better, Rand," he said cautiously. "We've probably eliminated all the dumb possibilities." He laughed nervously.

Randy made no response. Neil had a nagging feeling this wasn't so much about their impending doom as something personal directed at him.

"You feel like eating?" David asked Randy.

Randy's dark eyes came up and met David's with no sign of rancor or bad will. They looked almost warm. "Could we just wait a minute? I really need to calm down. Anything I eat right now is going to come right back up."

Neil tested his theory. "Look at this," he said, holding up his bandaged hand.

Randy glanced at the bandage, not at Neil, then returned his gaze to the water without comment.

Neil was baffled. They hadn't even been together! How could he have pissed Randy off? If the younger guys hadn't been there, he would have asked what was wrong, but it might be something embarrassing, so he just kept quiet.

115

"You guys eat if you're hungry," Randy said to the water. "I'll catch up."

All three chorused extravagant protests. Neil thought at that particular moment, anyone would have opened a vein to please Randy, just because he was sulking. Neil felt a little envious. Whenever he tried to sulk, people usually didn't notice.

"Chloe likes you, too," Randy muttered.

Neil looked up. "Huh?"

"She likes you, too. She's always had a crush on you. So now you can be happy and stand on top of a wedding cake."

Neil looked to David and Terry for confirmation that Randy was being weird. They both shrugged.

At least now he's talking to me, Neil thought. "How do you know?"

Finally Randy made eye contact with Neil, an expression chillingly reminiscent of the rattlesnake. "Because *she* tells me things."

Neil knew something important was being said here. It was so important he didn't even dare take a minute and celebrate the fact that Chloe liked him. "Why didn't you tell me before?"

"She asked me not to. She thought you'd see her as a dumb little kid with a crush. I'm just telling you now because we're all dead men and you might as well go out happy."

Terry gasped.

"That's not funny." Neil sat up straighter, angry now.

Randy's eyes narrowed. "It's not my *job* to be funny, here."

Neil took a deep breath. "It's not your job to act like a jerk either. If you've got a problem with me dating your sister, why don't you come out and say so?"

"Because I don't have a problem with you dating my sister."

"Then what in the hell is your problem?" Neil shouted.

"Here we go again," Terry whined, running a hand through his hair.

"No, we don't," Randy said. "It really isn't worth it. My problem, Neil, is that you don't know what my problem is."

For some reason, David laughed.

Neil felt ganged up on. "I—"

"Don't worry about it," Randy said, sitting up and unzipping his pack. "Let's eat. I'm over it. I'm hungry."

Neil felt as if he was going to cry. He had to hold his breath for almost a minute to fight down the urge. But luckily, as usual, nobody seemed to notice.

———

For dinner they broke out Chloe's fried rice and Randy's Doritos. They sat in a circle around the Tupperware container, using the rice as a chip dip. The sky above the ceiling was a flaming red now, as the sun set. They were quiet for a while, settled into the rhythms of dipping and crunching. Neil listened to the rush of the stream and felt contented. "This is like being cavemen," he said.

"Did they have Tupperware?" Terry grinned.

"They had cave*women*!" David said. "Which is the main thing missing in this setup."

Neil was eating Chloe's home-cooked food, so for the moment he felt no such loneliness. He took a long drink of cold spring water, feeling it wash the pleasant burn of Chloe's chilies and spices all through his mouth. She liked him, too. All this time, sitting silently in the kitchen together, they had felt the same.

"I know what you mean, though," Terry said to Neil. "It's really . . . peaceful in here. If we weren't in a horrible situation, this would be like camping."

"You've never been camping," David said to Terry.

"I know, but I watch TV!"

"I never have either," Randy said.

"Really?" Neil asked.

"Hello?" Randy said. "I'm Jewish, remember? From Miami Beach? We only get to go to camp if we're fat. I'd love it, though. If we do get out of here alive, we should all do that sometime."

"Yeah," Neil said quickly, aware that this was Randy's way of making up.

"I wonder what's going on back home right now," David said.

"Thanks," Neil said. "We were almost feeling good there for a second."

"Well, excuse me," David said. "One of us has to be plugged into reality here. This is not a camping trip. This is a fucking death trap."

"Do you know what you remind me of?" Neil said to David. "Did you ever read *The Masque of the Red Death* in English class? You're the clock. Striking in every room. Whenever people start to feel good."

118

David waved a Dorito in Neil's face. "Am I supposed to pretend I don't know the situation?"

Randy put his hand in the air between Neil and David. "We're just trying to take a little break from reality, Sport. That's all. Just so we can digest our food."

"But we should be thinking," David said. "What we did today didn't work. We should be analyzing it and deciding what went wrong so we won't screw up tomorrow. Because, guys, we still have a couple more meals here, but then we're down to the scorpions and rattlesnakes."

Randy slumped. "He's right. Okay, Neil, swallow your food and chair another meeting."

"Well," Neil brandished his hand. "What I learned today is that I'm clumsy. And that two random tunnels—mine and Terry's—were basically circular. Did either of you end up back this way?" He looked at David and Randy in turn.

"Nope," Randy sliced the air with his hand. "I just had a straight line to nowhere. When I was halfway through my time, I turned around and came back."

"Yeah." David dropped his eyes.

"Okay, so two tunnels curved back on themselves and two tunnels went straight toward . . . something." Neil traced the patterns in the air with his fingers.

Terry spoke up. "Neil, you and I went further down this main tunnel before we branched off."

"So?"

Terry moved the rice aside and drew in the dirt with his finger. "We could start guessing that the tun-

119

nels close to this chamber go straight and the ones further out circle around." His diagram looked like a fountain.

"So," Randy pointed to the diagram. "If we pick the nearer tunnels, we might up the odds."

"Or," David said, "this could mean nothing. You're trying to draw a conclusion from four tunnels out of a hundred. This cave is so much bigger than we thought. This could be a sinkhole with tunnels that go all over Florida. There might be only one way out and . . . just by trial and error we wouldn't live long enough to find it!"

"Bong! Bong! Bong!" Neil said.

"I can't help it!" David cried. "It's the truth!"

"But it's not helpful!" Terry said. "Look, shouldn't we try either Randy's or David's tunnels tomorrow? Because we know they go somewhere?"

"We don't know that!" David said. "We just know they don't come back here. Our tunnels could have come to a dead end ten yards ahead of where we stopped." He leaned forward and drew over Terry's diagram. "These close tunnels could go straight for a long way and then curve back like the shorter ones. See? I mean, I'm sorry, but I have to say it again. The only way out might be the way we came in, and since we can't remember that—"

"We're all going to die!" Neil said.

"I have to speak up, don't I?" David's eyes were pleading.

"It's the way you do it!" Neil said. "It's, like, deep down you want the worst to happen."

"No!" Suddenly David looked very emotional. And very young. "Why would I want that?"

"Time out, time out," Randy said. "Let's just say David's right. There's only one way out and we don't have the time to find it. What else could we do?" As Randy was speaking, his whole face was suddenly covered with little points of light, like tiny rainbows. Neil thought he was going crazy and looked to the far wall, only to see more rainbows, millions of them dancing in little fragments over the smooth white calcite and the dark rock walls beyond. The stream and the pool pulsed like liquid opals. The other boys, all speckled like Easter eggs, were gazing at their own hands, each other, the walls. Then, one by one, they tipped their heads back and looked up at the ceiling.

"God!" Terry said.

It was the crystals. The slant of the setting sun had somehow angled in and directly struck the bank of crystals, igniting them so they glowed. Each one cast down concentric showers of prismatic light, like the patterns in a stained glass window.

The pool, reflecting all this, multiplied the effect and added a dancing, moving quality. It was like sitting inside a kaleidoscope. Neil blinked and shook his head, but the images were real. He felt a thrill. His heart beat fast.

"It must do this every day at this time," David whispered.

Neil was getting lost in it. He found by turning his head, he could create the illusion of fireworks all

121

around him. He raised his right hand and sparks seemed to fly off his fingertips.

"Maybe this is some kind of sign," Terry said.

"Get lost," David said, shoving him gently. Colors shifted across his face and arms like fish scales.

"We are lost," Terry giggled, shoving him back. "Listen to me. We were asking if there was another way out and *something made us all look up*. Maybe there's a way to climb up there and get out."

"Terry," David said. "That's a hundred feet up. This is just an illusion, just refraction. I don't think we should start getting all magical . . ."

Neil was barely listening. He just wanted to look and be lost in the colors. *How can things be so frightening and so beautiful at the same time?*

"Let's be magical for a second," Randy said. "What harm would it do? I mean we tried rational, David, and it just told us we're fucked. It seems like we're fairly free to try something different."

Terry was excited now, ripples of chartreuse and orange and purple flickering across his face. "Look at those calcite formations. They're full of ledges. They're almost like stairs. And higher up, all the stone is bumpy and ridgy. There's handholds and footholds. Someone who's a good climber, if he was careful, could do it. He could take a rope up there and then help the others. Which one of us is the best climber?"

David and Randy spoke in unison. "Neil."

Neil woke up a little at the sound of his name. He felt drunk, dizzy, as if he'd just stepped off a furious carnival ride. He cocked his head back and looked at the narrow opening, ringed by flaming crystals. The sky beyond was bloodred, streaked with purple. He felt as if he could reach right up and touch it.

TEN

Neil had been born with an impulse to climb. His mother told him she'd found him, at eighteen months, hanging by his hands from a towel rack in the bathroom. He felt the urge, right from the beginning, to always go up and out. His early childhood had been full of episodes involving trees, roofs and, once, the top bookshelves in the Ormond Beach Public Library.

The secret of climbing, Neil knew, was a special kind of intuition in the muscles themselves. The same ability had helped him earn a letter in wrestling in junior high. People attributed his success to his size, but it was his smart muscles. Whenever he was pinned, some part of his body would report in, sensing a spot where the opponent was weak and pressure could be applied. Slowly and surely, Neil would work on that spot until the tables were turned and he was the one on top. The other boys, he could see, had no muscle intuition. They flailed, raged, guessed. They lost. Neil had retired undefeated, bored by the lack of challenge.

124

Climbing was essentially the same skill, only more advanced. All the muscles had to report in every second and the balance had to be constantly adjusted. People thought climbing was about hanging on to things, but it was really about not falling. As a kid, Neil honed his skill on trees, privacy fences and the facades of public buildings. In PE, he was always the first one up the rope. On the playground he'd been a genius of the jungle gym. He made bets with other kids sometimes that he could climb any tree, even a palm. He never lost.

The height of his climbing career had come at age fourteen, when the whole family took a driving trip west. It was, in fact, the last vacation the whole family had taken together. In Colorado, Neil managed to talk his dad into taking him and David on a supervised rock-climbing expedition. Mimi wanted to go, too, but Mom said no. After a week of practice and training, a couple of guides took them, along with six other people, on a climb up a steep canyon wall, several hundred feet in the air. Here, among professionals, Neil's gifts stood out. When they reached the first resting ledge, all the other tourists were wheezing and sweating and amazed to be alive. He stood peacefully between the two guides, admiring the view of the canyon through tattered clouds. One of the guides gave him a little slap on the back. "You've done this before, haven't you, kid?"

It had been one of the best moments in Neil's life.

———

The rainbow effect had faded now and The Chamber was growing dim. The sky over the crevice was a deep violet. In a minute they would have to turn their flashlights on.

Neil peered into the shadows, analyzing his course. "I might be able to do it," he said. "Terry's right. I've got a good beginning on the calcite. I mean, it's probably as slippery as shit. It'll be like climbing porcelain, but look how it almost makes a diagonal stairway, right here." He pointed.

David turned on his flashlight and illuminated the area Neil was pointing to. The other boys frowned at it, concentrating, as if willing Neil to be right.

Neil took David's wrist and cocked it up to illuminate the area halfway up the wall. "Right here is where the trouble starts. Because the calcite gets sheer, so I have to switch to the cave wall itself and I don't see a good ledge to move off onto. The nearest one would be here"—he adjusted the light again— "but I can't spread my legs that far apart."

"Too bad we don't have Laura Wexler in here," Randy said.

David laughed. "If we had Laura Wexler in here, I wouldn't care that much about getting out." He looked at Neil. "Are you saying it's impossible?"

"Nothing is impossible," Neil said. "I just have to work it out. I could probably reach over and get that ledge with my hands, standing on the highest calcite ridge. I'd have to grab it, swing off and dangle and then get my feet up there. The limestone isn't slick, so I'd have a good grip. Does anybody have gloves?"

"Eagle Scout has gloves," Randy said. "I remember the inventory."

"Yes, I do." David lifted his chin slightly.

Neil tugged down on the bill of David's cap. "You're good for something every once in a while, even if you are annoying, kid. I'm not sure I want them. I might want to be able to feel things in my hands, but I'd like to have them in case I get sweaty. So the only bad thing is that little transition. After that the limestone would be fairly good all the way to the top." He adjusted the flashlight again to show how many ledges he could see. "The only scary part is that one transition. It's not good to have your weight dangling like that when you're seventy feet up. If I made a mistake, I'd fall straight down, feet first. I could break my back."

"Is there a different route?" David asked.

"No," Neil said. "This one is too perfect. I have to go where the calcite leads me. It's a perfect route with one little problem. Anything else I do would be more risky."

"How big is that opening?" Terry asked. "Are we sure a big guy like Neil can fit through it? Maybe somebody scrawnier should do it."

"You volunteering?" Randy asked him.

Terry laughed. "You're pretty thin."

Randy laughed back. "Yeah, and I can't climb my way out of a deep hammock. David?"

"Forget it. I've been rock climbing with Neil, and he leaves me in the dust. But we should try to figure out if his shoulders fit that hole."

"Oh, come on!" Neil said. "You can always screw around and get through a tight place if you have to. It looks big enough to me. How big do you think I am?"

"Do you know your suit size?" Terry asked. His father owned a chain of men's clothing stores.

"Forty-four long." Neil laughed.

"Jeez! You're huge. You'd need a hole about twenty inches long and maybe ten inches wide."

Everyone looked up.

"Yeah . . . ," Randy said. "That's just about what it looks like."

"Just about won't work if it's too small by a few inches," David said.

"I will make it work," Neil said patiently. "It's close enough!"

"Yeah, you love to beat up on rocks!" David said. "Which brings up another question. What about your hand?"

"My hand is fine," Neil said. "Do you want me to smack you to prove it?"

"Neil," David said. "You're talking about how you have to hang by your hands for a few seconds. If one of your hands hurts too much, you might let go!"

"I can ignore pain when I want to," Neil said. Which was true. When he hadn't been winning bets about tree climbing, he'd been winning bets about holding his hands over lighted candles.

"His knee is hurt, too, remember," Terry said.

Neil waved his hand. "Enough of this. Give me the gloves and the rope and let's get out of here."

"Wrong, Man of Steel!" Randy said. "It's getting dark and everybody's tired. I want you doing this in the morning, when maybe there's a fifty-fifty chance you won't screw it up."

"No, listen!" Neil said. He looked at his watch. "It's only seven! If we got out now, we could drive home in two hours and be back home by nine! We could sleep in our own beds tonight!"

Randy turned to David. "He's going crazy. Say something negative."

"How do we even know your car is still there?" David obliged.

"God, I hate all of you!" Neil shouted. "For two cents I'd strangle every one of you! Why the *hell* do you want to spend an extra night trapped in this fucking coffin if we don't have to?"

Randy took a handful of Neil's hair and pulled his head back. "See up there, Big Shot? It's *dark*. It's *night*. You're expecting us to put all our hopes on a frazzled, tired, scraped-up, bitched-out lunatic, climbing a hundred feet of wet, slippery rocks in the dark? You see our point? We'd just like to up the odds a little on our final chance of getting out of here alive. Can you see that?"

Neil shook loose and glared at him.

"Neil, I know how you feel," David said. "I mean, I know we'd be in less trouble if we could get home tonight, but we have to face it. We're already fucked. Mom started getting crazy hours ago and we both know it."

"Is that his problem?" Randy asked David. "Neil,

are you seriously worried about your mommy being mad at you? We're in a life-and-death thing here and you're afraid you'll get a spanking?"

"It's not like that," David said before Neil could respond. "I know how he feels. You just have to be in our family. If you do something dumb like this . . . they never really . . . they treat you different from then on." He looked away. "Forever," he whispered.

"Don't think about that," Neil said. "We've got enough trouble."

"I'm not thinking about it!" David shouted. "I'm never allowed to think about it! Don't you think I know that?"

Terry touched David's arm. "Let's stay on the current problem. Neil, you know we're right. You look totally exhausted right now. And your hand would be a little bit more healed by morning. I know it must be awful for someone like you, to be stuck inside here overnight—"

"What do you mean, someone like him?" Randy said.

Terry looked at Neil. "I'm sorry," he said, already starting to cringe in case Neil lashed out.

"Thanks," Neil said. "Thanks a whole hell of a lot."

Randy closed his eyes briefly. This was usually a sign he was waiting for a wave of homicidal rage to pass. "Why," he asked quietly, "can't Neil stand to spend the night here? If it wouldn't be too much trouble to TELL ME!" The last words came up in such a sudden roar that Terry actually skittered back from Randy a few inches.

"This is just great!" Neil said to Terry.

"I'm sorry!" Terry whined.

David put his hand on Terry's back as if to steady him. "You're having some kind of problem with being closed in, aren't you?" he said to Neil.

An exhalation rolled out of Neil like a wave. "Yeah."

"That's how he hurt his hand," Terry said, as if he couldn't control himself now. "He was having a fit when I found him, pounding on the wall."

"I knew it," David said.

"*I* didn't," Randy snarled. "But then, of course—"

"He's exaggerating!" Neil pleaded. "I'm really all right! I'm fine!"

"Yeah, you're just fine, Neil!" Randy said. Neil could almost see the anger coming off him, like the heat shimmers off a car. "You're always fine, aren't you? That's the main thing with you, how fine you are. Someday I'll go to a cemetery and there will be your headstone and it'll say, 'No, no, really, I'm fine!'"

"Randy," Neil said. "I know you're really mad at me. You've been mad at me all day and it's getting worse and worse, but I've got to tell you. I need a little help here. I'm stupid. I don't understand what the problem is. I don't see how you can expect me to fix—"

"You don't just 'fix' everything! You—oh, just forget it."

No one spoke. The Chamber was getting dark. They could hardly see each other's faces now. David propped his flashlight up, lamp-style. Neil noticed it was getting colder, too. He could see very clearly why wolves wanted to howl at night.

131

"I just had a really terrible thought!" David said.

Everyone laughed. Even Randy. "Well, by all means," Randy said, "share it with the group."

David looked grim. "We don't have anything to use for toilet paper."

Everyone laughed again, with a slightly hysterical edge.

"Oh, god," Randy said, his face registering real fear for the first time that day.

Neil thought of Baudelaire. But he was almost to the point of being unable to speak.

"Maybe nobody will have to . . . do that," Terry said.

"I have to," Randy said. "I had to the minute David brought the stupid subject up. All right, Neil, start climbing!"

Neil laughed. "Don't panic, boys, I've got paper."

"Thank you, God!" Randy said. "But why didn't you tell us you had toilet paper when we took inventory?"

Neil was rummaging in his pack. "I don't have toilet paper. I have poetry." He realized he didn't care what they thought of him anymore. It was too late anyway. They knew he was crazy, they knew he was scared. Randy seemed to think he was a shit. He had nothing to lose anymore. It was kind of a good feeling.

"Poetry?" Randy asked, grabbing the book and examining it. "This is just getting to be too much. What planet are you from and what have you done with my friend Neil?"

David took the book from Randy and examined it. "This is weird," he said.

"What's weird about it?" Neil asked. "I thought all of you would be bringing poetry today. I thought maybe later we'd have a little reading! And some tea!"

"He has flipped," Randy said. He took the book back from David again. "Nobody make any sudden moves." He picked up David's flashlight and scanned the cover, which featured a naked man and woman being swallowed by a sea serpent. "Is this *dirty* poetry?" he asked Neil, obviously struggling for some logical explanation. "Is it a jerk-off book?"

"It's Charles Baudelaire," Neil said. "He's French. The symbolist school. Mostly they're poems about despair. That used to be a little hobby of mine." He couldn't remember ever feeling better in his life. What could they do to him? It was like the moment in *Alice's Adventures in Wonderland* when Alice realized that all her enemies were just playing cards.

Randy closed the book. "Neil, I'm sorry," he said. "If I'd known how really batshit you were, I never would have been mad at you. Obviously you're not responsible." He looked at the others. "Guys, what do you think of this? Our lives depend on a guy who likes to read despair poetry written by some French fag!"

"Can I see it?" Terry asked.

Randy handed Terry the book.

Neil felt free, as if some dam had broken inside him and tidal waves were rolling out. "I carry it with me wherever I go. I'm actually afraid to go anyplace

133

without it. I take it to school. I take it to basketball games. I take it to the beach, wrapped in a towel. It's like one of those blankets little kids carry around. It used to make me feel protected or safe or something. So!" He looked at the three astonished faces gazing at him. "Do I win? Am I the craziest one here? Did any of you ever, in your wildest dreams, guess how fucked up I was? I bet not!" He felt like doing cartwheels.

David's expression suddenly softened. "How long have you been doing this? Carrying it around?"

Neil held his eyes. "Two years."

David's eyes were steady, too. "Since the funeral."

"Yes." He didn't care. He wanted it all to come out. He wanted to confess. Then he realized Randy didn't know what they were talking about. He turned to him.

Randy stood up. "This is all really interesting but I do have to go to the bathroom. Excuse me?" He took the Baudelaire from Terry, who'd turned on his flashlight and been reading with interest. "Talk about anything you want when I'm gone. The fire, the funeral, whatever. I'll cough real loud before I come back, so you'll have time to shut up again."

"No," Neil said. "I'm sorry. Let me tell you—"

"It can wait," Randy said coldly. "It's waited this long." He walked away, his left hand clenching the poetry book so hard it was crushing the pages.

Neil could feel David and Terry staring at him, even though he was afraid to look at them. "I guess he's mad because I've kept so many secrets from him."

"Well, duh," said David.

Neil's elation had melted away. He felt bone weary all of a sudden. His spine sagged. He leaned back on his elbows, feeling every ache and pain from the whole long agonizing day. "Why does that make him angry?" he asked. "I was sparing him. Did he want to hear me pissing and moaning all about this horrible shit that happened to us? Why would anybody want that?"

"So he could *know* you," David said. His voice was kind.

Even breathing seemed painful. Neil stretched out on his side, pillowing his head with his elbow. David and Terry both looked as if they pitied him. They were the experts here. They knew everything about friendship. Neil realized he didn't know anything. "I guess I thought if he knew me, he wouldn't like me," he said faintly. "Doesn't that make sense?"

Terry spoke up. "No. If nobody knows you, how can you tell yourself anybody really likes you?"

Neil shifted again. Flat on his back, not caring if he got dirt in his hair. Eyes closed. He felt as if maybe somewhere deep inside his body he was crying but it just wasn't coming to the surface. "I used to tell myself all kinds of things," he whispered.

ELEVEN

Neil opened his eyes and saw stars. For a second he was able to feel postnap relaxation in every muscle. Then he realized he was seeing the belt of Orion through an ironing-board-shaped crevice in a ceiling of rock. He sat up, muscles springing back into the clench he'd held all day. "Why did you guys let me fall asleep?" he shouted.

Two silhouettes by the pool swiveled, dim as ghosts. Neil could tell by size and shape it was Terry and David, sitting with a flashlight propped between them. "We thought we could handle all the excitement around here by ourselves," David answered. "And you were so exhausted—"

Neil stood up, feeling dizzy. "I was not exhausted!" He felt irrationally angry, as if they'd let the darkness in. As if he, Neil, could have kept it out by staying awake. "Where's Randy?" he asked.

"Well . . . ," Terry said. "We were just discussing that. He went to the boys' room over an hour ago. So either he thought your poetry book was really interesting or there's something wrong with that fried rice."

"Why didn't somebody go after him?" Neil

136

took an aggressive step toward Terry. His adrenaline was stuck and he knew it. "How do you know he didn't get bitten by a snake or a scorpion or god knows what else crawls around in Florida caves? Are you guys stupid? What time is it?"

"Nine o'clock," said David. "Calm down. We were just about to wake you up and ask you—"

"Can't you handle anything by yourselves? You have to wake me up to go check on a guy in the bathroom?" Neil could hear his own shrillness.

David was getting flushed. "We didn't know what to do! You don't just invade a guy's privacy when he —he's *your* friend. Anyway, he was pissed off when he left, so we figured he was just taking a time-out."

Remembering that Randy was angry added fuel to Neil's anger. "Well, you don't just 'figure' when you're in an emergency like this! We have to stay together and look out for each other! Don't you know anything?"

"I guess not!" David shouted back. "I guess I just don't have your sterling leadership qualities!"

Neil thought he heard sarcasm. He was panting now, in a fury. "This is how things go wrong!" he said. "When you don't pay attention!"

"You were asleep, you fucker!" David shot back. "What kind of paying attention is that?"

Neil was trying to think of an answer to that when David's voice suddenly rose to a wail. "Every time you get upset, you think you can dump on me. You're always yelling at me, like I caused every disaster in the world! I just did one wrong thing in my whole life and—"

"It was a *big* thing!" Neil's voice roared out, words he hadn't planned.

David screamed back. "I *know* it was a big thing!" His body slumped, maybe crying, maybe just defeated.

Neil managed to stop himself from saying anything else, clenching his fists, breathing hard. In the shadows he saw Terry reach out to David. David leaned away.

"I'm going to look for Randy," Neil said. He picked up his flashlight and flicked it on. "Maybe he needs cheering up, too." He hoped that sounded like the apology it was meant to be.

Randy was not in the boys' room but just outside the main chamber, a slumped figure by the spring. From his position, it looked as if he'd been holding his head in the stream of water and then fallen asleep or passed out or . . .

Panicking, Neil went down hard on his bad knee, jostling Randy with one hand and shining the light in his face. To his relief, Randy brought up both hands, thumping Neil like a volleyball, making him totter and fall back on his ass. "Jerk!" Randy said, but his voice had a funny childlike edge.

Neil shone the light directly in Randy's eyes, looking for clues.

Both hands came up again, trying to hide and deflect. "What are you, a cop? Quit that!"

"You've been crying," Neil said. He'd never seen Randy actually cry. He'd seen wavering, especially last year when Randy's father had walked out, but never a full plunge off the cliff. Randy always stopped himself before things got too sticky. He and Neil were alike in that, disdainful of theatrics. Terrified of pity.

Randy hiked his knees up and dangled his arms over them. This created a crisscross network of dark limbs that obscured his face. "Fuck off," he said. "Go back in the living room and scream at your brother some more. I can feel bad all by myself."

Neil rearranged himself on the dirt floor, to show he was settling in. "I'm glad you're just in despair," he said. "I was afraid I'd have to help you with some kind of *bathroom* problem."

A low chuckle escaped the tangle of arms and legs.

Neil counted off a few beats. "Wanna talk about it?"

"No."

Not much maneuvering room there. Still, Neil had a few more Randy-manipulating tricks up his sleeve. One thing that usually worked was to spout a lot of nonsense. It played to Randy's need to keep the record straight.

"It's just your turn," Neil said in a soothing voice he knew would make his friend's flesh crawl. "We're all frightened. It's only natural."

"It's not *that*!" Randy snapped.

Now the most effective weapon. Total silence. Neil had perfected all these techniques last year. But tonight it wasn't working. Randy let the uncomfortable silence tick on. Neil was alarmed. He'd seen Randy in pretty bad shape but never so broken he didn't care whether Neil understood or not.

139

"I don't want to flatter myself," Neil said cautiously. "But is this partly about me? I mean, we were having some kind of fight before. . . ."

Another bitter chuckle.

Maybe playing dumb was bad strategy after all. "I guess this is about how you thought you knew me these past two years and now you're hearing stuff you never heard before and you wonder what kind of nut your best friend is."

Randy's voice was low but struck the air like flint. "Do I have a best friend?"

Neil felt a jolt in the stomach that kept him from speaking for several seconds. The spring beside them filled in the gap, splashing and bubbling. The cave seemed much colder now, as night came on. Neil felt an impulse to get up and run from the conversation he knew was coming, but where could he go? Back toward David, where things were even worse. Neil felt like a bad chess player, hemmed in by his own stupid moves. He tried a line that sometimes worked with girls. "It's not you, Randy, it's me."

The laugh again, a flat, sarcastic single note. *Try again, jerk.*

"There were a million times I wanted to tell you this stuff," Neil pleaded. "But—"

"But what?" Randy shifted, dropping the arm-and-leg shield, leaning forward. "I want to know. For two years I was pouring my guts on the floor in front of you, telling you stuff about my dad that I've never told anyone. Anyone. And you're so superior, you've got a fucking *death* in the family, I guess, and your brother burned your house down *two months* before you met me, but nothing! You're so fucking superior you don't need to—"

"I did need to!" Neil said. "I couldn't!"

"Why?"

"I don't know. It was *stuck.*" Neil slapped the dirt floor, raising a cloud of dust. There. That was the truth. It didn't make any sense, but it was the truth.

"Stuck!"

"It's stuck!" Neil insisted. "I can't talk to anybody about it. Not even the people in my family. My throat closes up. I can't think of words. My brain shuts down. I can't help it. Don't hold this against me, Randy. Feel sorry for me. It's like . . . I don't even think I'm a human being. I think I'm just some kind of . . . idea." He knew he was raving now. That didn't make any sense. The truth never did.

Randy's voice softened. "Just answer questions. Who was it that died?"

Just answer questions. My sister. The answer to that question is: my sister. Neil felt his diaphragm lift painfully. The muscles in his face contorted. "My sister," he gagged. "Mimi." He covered his face with his hands, heaving.

Randy's hand touched him lightly on the arm.

———

Neil only cried for a couple of minutes, but when he was done, he felt as if he'd lost twenty pounds and been cured of a raging fever.

Randy sat patiently, neither hovering, nor ignoring,

just observing quietly. "Which one of these poems do you want to blow your nose on?" he asked.

Neil coughed a laugh. "Doesn't matter."

"So?" Randy said. "Did your sister die in the fire?"

"Yuh." Neil blew his nose on Baudelaire and wiped his face with the hem of his T-shirt.

"How old?"

"Nine."

Randy made a sympathetic noise. "I'd go crazy if something happened to Chloe or Rachel."

Neil laughed sadly. "Well?"

"I'd say you and David are doing pretty well, considering. So he started the fire, right? I'm having to piece this all together from the little revelations of the day."

"Yuh."

"So that's why David's always knocking himself out to be perfect and win you over—"

"Win me—"

"But I still don't see why *you're* all plugged up. What are you hiding? Who are you hiding from?"

Neil leaned back against the cave wall, feeling the bumpy coldness through his shirt. All his muscles ached. His brain seemed to ache. "I've always been like that. That's just me. I'm a coward, I guess."

"I know that's not true. Is there part of this you still aren't telling?"

"Nothing," Neil said. "I told you everything. And I feel better. I really feel much better. They're going to be wondering . . ." He looked off into the darkness toward the main chamber.

"How did the fire start?" Randy said.

Neil's brain cut out like a cheap outboard motor. "What?"

"Do you know how David started the fire?"

Neil nodded. But of course Randy couldn't see that.

"Hello?" Randy said.

"I can't," Neil said after a minute.

"You can't tell me? Is it a government secret?"

"I can't." Neil felt as if the ground under him was whirling. He repositioned his hands in the dirt so he wouldn't fall or fly off into space.

Randy let a few seconds go by. "Neil, I think some part of this is your fault. Or you think it is."

If I just don't do anything, Randy will disappear and this cave will go away and I'll never have to say it. And if I never say it, it didn't happen.

Randy leaned forward, the flashlight making a halo around his dark form. "Neil, you have to tell me. Believe me, you can't get rid of anything unless you say it to someone. Just blurt it out and don't think about it."

Neil was gagging. "Can't."

Randy sighed. A few more seconds went by. Then Randy leaned forward, picked up the flashlight and snapped it off. Everything disappeared. The sound of the stream seemed to increase in volume. "Try it now," Randy said.

Neil opened his mouth. Air was moving up and down his throat normally. He began to speak in a flat, monotone that reminded him of interviews on *60 Minutes*, where the person's face is distorted by colored squares. "I wanted to smoke pot," he began.

143

"You?"

"Yes. I was sick of my image. We'd had a party at the end of the basketball season and some of the guys, the varsity guys, were doing that—not the whole team but some guys. And when they offered it to me, I could hear myself giving this speech like Captain America and I thought, *you jerk*."

The darkness chuckled. "You know I gave up all that stuff when I left Miami and moved up to Ormond."

"I know you did."

"Mostly because of your good example, Captain America."

"Yeah, well. After that party, I just kept feeling like a schmuck. And I wanted to just smoke one joint in my stupid life, so I could say at the next party, 'Oh, of course I've tried it, but it's not for me.' You know?"

"You didn't want to be a virgin."

"Right. So over the summer I found a guy."

"Guys like that are easy to find."

"Yes. And I bought one joint, already rolled because I thought I might be too stupid to even roll it right."

The darkness laughed again.

"One joint, Randy. Just one. But then I was chickenshit about it. I kept putting it off. I had it under the bed, in this box where I keep stuff . . . you know, magazines and things. . . ."

"Yeah, we all have a place like that."

"Well, apparently, little brothers know where those places are. So the rest is obvious. Mom and Dad were out. Mimi was asleep in her room. I was at work. So

144

my brother must have found this thing and smoked it. He says he got very, very stoned."

"That doesn't make sense, on one joint. It must have been weird stuff. How well did you know the guy who sold it to you?"

"Not at all. Great, more to feel guilty about. Anyway, he fell asleep or something and it burned the bedspread and went right on to the curtains. David said he was so wasted he could hardly get out of the house. I mean, I guess he knew the house was on fire but he was just watching it happen, saying, 'wow!' or something. I don't know. They found him on the front lawn with sparks showering down on him. The shirt he was wearing was covered with little burns. He was full of smoke. They had to take him to the hospital and give him oxygen and stuff. And somehow he had apparently just forgotten all about Mimi. Just forgot she was in the house."

"It could happen. You've been drunk a few times, Neil. You know what it's like when you're . . . impaired."

"I know. He thinks I blame him, but I don't. He wouldn't have had that stuff if I hadn't put it in the house. This is all my fault. Everything is all my fault." Neil felt numb now. Lightheaded. He reached forward and turned the flashlight back on. "Good ghost story?" he asked Randy.

"You and David have never really talked about this, have you?"

Neil shrugged. "What's there to say?"

"What's there to say? Are you kidding? Do you see your brother, tiptoeing around you? Scrambling for a

145

handkerchief before you sneeze? He's waiting for you to tell him what you just told me. I'll bet he has no idea you think it's your fault."

"Randy, he was there. He knows it was my fault as much as I do. Do I have to let him shove my face right in it?"

"I don't think he would, but even if he did, it would break up this . . . logjam you guys have going. Isn't it worse holding your breath for two years? It's always been painful to watch you guys, but I never quite knew why. Do your parents know all this?"

"What do you mean?"

"They know how David started the fire?"

"Sure. He told them."

"Do they know it was your stuff?"

Neil closed his eyes. "No."

"He let them think it was his stuff?" Randy's voice grew strident.

"Yes," Neil whispered.

"What kind of a brother are you! You're letting David take the rap for this?"

"I told you I was a coward!" Neil shot back, loud enough, he realized, for David and Terry to hear in the main chamber. He pictured them trying to put the outcry in a context, like little kids listening to fragments of their parents' fights. "Listen," Neil said in a softer voice. "I know it's wrong, but . . . Mom and Dad never forgave him. They've shut him out. I mean, they aren't openly cruel . . . they don't say anything to him about it, but they aren't warm to him anymore. We used to be a really close family before this

146

happened. Now they just don't . . . reach out to him anymore. It's horrible to watch. And I'm scared of that happening to me."

The stream filled a few seconds of silence. Neil got up and leaned over the spring, letting the cold water hit his face. He shook himself like a dog and slumped down again, a little closer to Randy. He felt all alone.

"Neil, you're doing the same thing to him. If what you say is true, all you and David have left is each other."

"It's too late. Everything is wrecked. You can't go back."

"But you're not going forward either. Listen, talk to him now. Tonight. God knows we don't have anything else to do. I'll take Terry off on a scorpion hunt or something."

"You don't understand."

"You're right, I don't. Only you and David understand this and that's why you have to talk to each other."

Neil had been watching the spring. Now he looked at Randy's dimly lit face. "Now I see why I never talk to you," he complained. "Look, let's just get out of this horrible situation we're in and then maybe—"

"What if we don't get out?"

"What kind of a thing is that to say?"

"Neil, I'm just giving you back what you've been giving me for two years. What did you keep saying to me, over and over? Tell your father how you feel. Tell your father how you feel."

"Yeah. And now you think your father avoids you completely."

147

"But it's honest, Neil. Before we were choking on our own politeness. We were trying to act like we still liked each other. The point is, he really wanted to be rid of us, and I can't respect a man like that. And now we both know that, because we fought it out. He may not like me anymore. But the son of a bitch knows me. He knows what I stand for and he knows how I feel. I mean, maybe you and David will decide you hate each other. But at least you won't be choking to death on all the stuff you haven't said."

Neil drew his finger through the dirt. He drew a line, then a parallel line. Then he joined them to make a box. "Maybe I'm scared he'll never forgive me."

"That would be better than what he's doing to himself now. He's taking all the blame to keep you clean in his mind. And you're letting him."

"Randy, haven't we got enough going on just trying to stay alive in here? Can't this wait?"

Randy paused for just a second. "Were there any things you wanted to tell Mimi? But you thought they could wait?"

Neil's spine sagged. A heavy weight somewhere in his chest was pulling him down. The tears flowed out of him easily this time. He didn't resist them. Over his own muffled groans he heard Randy, methodically tearing out another page of Baudelaire.

10:00 P.M., SATURDAY

By the time Neil and Randy felt ready to rejoin the other boys, it was ten o'clock. Terry and David were squatting by the pool, Terry training his flashlight on something David was doing.

"You guys!" Randy called out to announce their arrival. "We gotta get out of here! We're missing *Baywatch*."

David turned around and grinned, then looked at Neil. He picked up his flashlight and turned it on, shining it in Neil's face. "What's the matter with *you*?"

Neil had held his face in the cold spring for five full minutes but it hadn't done any good. He had one of those complexions that give everything away. "I'll tell you in a minute," he said. "What are you doing?"

David was tying one end of his rope to a large, flat stone. "Well, we got bored with you guys gone so long." He glanced up at Terry, smirking. "How long were they in the boys' room together?"

Terry smiled nastily. Payback, Neil thought, and they had a right to it. "It was like a whole hour!"

149

David gave the knot a hard jerk. "A whole hour in the bathroom together," he said, shaking his head. "And you know, Terry. This morning they were making jokes about you and me. Weren't they?"

"Ha, ha, very funny, stop right there," Randy said, giving them a mild parody of his dangerous look. "Neil and I were doing rugged, manly things, weren't we, Neil?"

"We were bench-pressing and talking about how we shave," Neil said. "So what are you guys doing? It kind of looks like you're going to keelhaul somebody."

"Well," Terry said. "When we got tired of trying to hear what you guys were fighting about, David started showing me how to skip rocks in the pool—"

"We have limited recreation facilities in here," David interrupted.

"I did it, too," Terry said. "Didn't I?"

"It's not that big of an accomplishment, Ter," David told him. "But yeah, you were doing it. And we started talking about how deep this pool is." He tugged at his knot, testing it.

"So then we started dropping stones in and shining our lights down there," Terry said. "To try and see—"

"But you can't see the bottom," David concluded. "I even stained one of the rocks with Betadine to make it show up better but . . . it always disappears. The water is very clear, so this is a deep pool."

"I saw an episode of *Tales from the Crypt* like this," Randy said. "This guy's swimming pool turned out to be the doorway to hell."

"I saw that one!" Terry said. "He was a Hollywood producer."

"Anyway!" David said. "I'm gonna find out exactly how deep it is. I've got a hundred feet of rope here and I'm going to drop this rock like a—what do they call it?"

"Plumb line," Neil said. "But you're not going to do that. We need that rope to get out of here tomorrow. Untie it."

"I thought of that," David said. "But see? I've got this hook on the other end and I'm just going to attach it to some big, dead weight." He reached over and inserted the hook in Neil's belt loop. "There."

"You're a riot tonight, aren't you?" Neil said.

David made his face earnest and sincere. "I'll be careful, but you have to let me do it. It's driving me crazy not knowing how deep this pool is."

"I don't know," Neil said. "I don't like the idea of playing around with our lifeline."

"I've got another rope, remember?" Randy said.

"I know," Neil argued. "But yours is a nasty, scratchy hemp rope with no hook that's going to hurt my hands. And it's shorter than this one." He turned to David. "You can use Randy's rope for your science experiments, but leave the good one for me."

"Okay." David gestured to Randy, who rummaged in his pack. David began picking at the formidable knot he'd tied. He kept his eyes down as he asked, "So what *were* you guys doing all that time?"

"You already know, don't you?" Neil said. "You can see my face. I got upset."

David looked up. "About what?"

Neil felt edgy all over again. But there was something different this time. This time he had an urge to talk and let the edginess out, instead of trying to smother it. "Are you sure you want to go into it?" he asked.

David's eyes were fixed on Neil as David took the rope from Randy. "Yeah."

"Terry and I can leave—" Randy began.

Neil held up his hand. "I was telling Randy about the fire." The edginess became a surge. He almost felt high.

"Oh. Okay." David ducked his head. He knotted rope furiously. It was hard to tell in the light, but he seemed to be blushing.

Neil leaned forward, feeling almost aggressive. "I had never told Randy anything about it."

David swallowed visibly. "Uh-huh." His fingers slipped on the knot. He repositioned them and tugged angrily.

"You and I have never talked about it either," Neil said. He was shaking now, but determined to push through this.

David's response was a heartbreaking attempt at laughter. "What's there to say?"

"Don't do this to him now!" It was such a deep, commanding voice, Neil had to look twice to make sure it had come from Terry.

"Stay out of it!" Randy said to Terry. "This is between them!"

David seemed to be losing touch. He looked

blankly, in turn, at each person who had spoken. Then he turned his eyes back to Neil, pleading. "What do you want from me? Do you want me to say how sorry I am? Do I really have to say that? She was my sister, too. Do you think I wanted—"

"Stop it, stop it," Neil said. "You're babbling. I don't want to blame you or pick on you. I just think that after two years, we should be able to—"

"I'll never be able to talk about it!" David said, staring maniacally down at his tied-up rock. "So just forget it!"

"But . . ."

David's eyes filled with tears. "What good is that supposed to do? It's bad enough that it happened. I don't think people should just rake up every horrible thing and torture themselves with it!"

Neil heard their mother talking. "But I think we're both scared of what the other one is going to say. And it's pushed us apart, you know? Sometimes I think we avoid each other because—"

"What's this we?" David looked up, wet eyes blazing. "We aren't doing that! You do that! You decided not to have anything to do with me. You're the one who went out as soon as it happened and found yourself another friend. . . ." He swung his arm in Randy's direction like a jib. Randy swerved to avoid being hit. "So you wouldn't have to hang out with me anymore! If you're trying to tell me you're finally ready to forgive me, fine. That's great. I'll take that. I've been waiting two years for that. Or maybe this is because you think we won't get out of here alive and you're just trying to settle everything up. I don't know. But don't act like I ever pushed you off, because it was all on your side and I've just been waiting around like a *jerk* for you to tell me everything's okay again!" When David finished this speech, he was panting. His chest heaved. Randy and Terry were both perfectly still and alert, like soldiers in a trench trying to anticipate the next round of gunfire.

Neil was confused. "No," he said.

David looked up again, angry. "No what?"

"You . . . I . . ." Neil turned to Randy. "Tell him."

"You can tell him a lot better than I can," Randy said in the kind of patient voice kindergarten teachers use.

"Why do you guys even have to do this?" Terry wailed. "Why can't you be nice to each other and leave it alone?"

"That's what they've been doing and look at them!" Randy said. "David's exploding and Neil's . . . imploding."

David turned his wrath on Randy. "God! What are you, family counseling?"

"No, but that's what you should have had as soon as this thing happened!" Randy waved his hand in the small space between them. "And back off, too, because if you swing your hand near my face one more time, you won't get it back!"

"Randy's right," Neil said to David. "Mom and Dad are great but this whole plan they came up with about putting the past behind us—it didn't work! We both

154

know that. You don't know how I feel and I don't know how you feel and we don't know how Mom and Dad feel and we're all just guessing and treating each other like company and the only way to fix it is to just say whatever we want and let it happen. If we decide we hate each other, then at least we'll know. But the suspense is too much for me. I can't take it anymore."

"It's okay to talk to each other, but why can't you do it nicely?" Terry said.

Randy turned to him. "Because the truth isn't always nice."

No one spoke for a minute. The drip of water had a richer, more musical sound at night, Neil thought. It was soothing, even in the midst of all this. He felt his breathing slow down.

David had picked up the rock and was holding it in his lap with both hands. He looked at Neil. "Okay. What is it you want to say to me?"

Neil felt almost peaceful. "I've never blamed you for what happened. I blamed myself." Neil paused for David to react, but he didn't; he just stared at Neil, breathing hard. It looked as if he didn't believe him. "I bought the stuff. I put the stuff in our house. You were just a kid. You were curious. What happened was an accident. You didn't mean to set a fire. You didn't mean to . . . leave her there. . . ." His voice broke a little.

David's body slumped. "But I didn't even think of her. I didn't remember her. All I thought of was myself. I just thought, *get out*. I was so *stupid*!" His voice,

155

which had been low and defeated, rose to a scream so suddenly it made Terry flinch. The word *stupid* echoed all around them.

"You weren't stupid," Neil said. "You were high. And it was my fault you were high."

"Does this whole thing have to be somebody's fault?" Randy asked. "Don't you guys know about shit happening? Maybe you don't. You're all so careful and perfect—your whole family—that you probably got the idea somewhere you can control the universe. So when something goes wrong—"

"This is a big something!" David said. "This is death!"

"Well, here's a flash, David," Randy said. "Death happens to everybody, whether they floss or not. And you'll go crazy someday if you keep trying to be perfect, like that will ward off all the bad things that might happen to you in your life."

"He's right," Neil said.

Randy turned to Neil. "And you're exactly the same way! Look, ask me and Terry. We can be objective. You guys did a little misdemeanor thing and it had felony consequences. That's what happened. But you didn't mean for it to. Neither one of you is bad or stupid or a killer or anything. I think if you'd both let yourselves off the hook, you could be nicer to each other."

"I agree with all that," Terry said quietly.

"I do, too," Neil said.

"Yeah?" David was actually sneering at Neil. "That's nice. But it's a lie, isn't it? You know you don't mean it." He blinked several times to fight back tears. "The

156

minute it happened, Neil, I could see in your face how you felt about me. If we're supposed to tell the truth, why don't we really do it? If you really don't blame me for Mimi's death, why have you been treating me like shit for two years? You know you have. You look away from me whenever I come into a room. I had to beg to come along today. You can't even say my name. You always call me 'kid' or say, 'my brother' like I live in Cleveland or something. Tell me that's not true! You're just like Mom and Dad. You treat me like I'm a ghost, like I died in the fire, too. Admit it!"

Neil's body felt battered. He had felt David's words almost as blows on his chest. "In a way, that's true," he admitted. "But I don't do it because I'm angry or because I blame you for what happened."

"Then why?" David's eyes were fearless.

Neil dropped his. "I don't know." He stared at the dirt. All this emotion spent and nothing solved. Mother was right, after all.

"Well, I'm sure glad we did this!" Terry said bitterly. "It was pretty boring, just wondering if we were going to die. Now we've had all this fun, too. Maybe Randy could talk about how his dad abandoned them now, or I could show you a few of my recent bruises—"

"Okay, okay," Neil said. "I'm sorry." He wished he could either deny his avoidance of David or explain it. But he couldn't do either.

David looked up, rocking his body back and forth in little jabs. His jaw was clenched. "You've said everything you wanted to say?"

Neil sighed. "I guess so."

David picked up the end of his rope. "I need to tie this to something—"

"Here." Neil took the rope and tied it around his ankle. He began to babble, trying to shift the mood. "This is the way pirates used to execute people. Actually, they tied the prisoner's ankle to a weighted bucket and made him kick it overboard. That's where the expression *kick the bucket* comes from."

David, who was usually amused by such stories, remained stone-faced as he tied a rather tight, hard knot around Neil's ankle with that nasty, scratchy hemp rope.

But Terry was fascinated. "Is that true?"

"He makes up stories like that all the time," David said. "He's a born liar."

"But this is true!" Neil insisted.

"He was such a liar as a kid," David went on. "We were in a shopping center once and he grabbed me and pointed to this grungy-looking couple and he says, 'Oh, god! Don't look! That's our real parents!'"

Neil chuckled. "I remember that."

David positioned himself to drop the rock. "And all day he kept adding to the story. These people were the Schwartzes. They'd put us up for adoption when we were really little, but Neil could remember it. I believed him after a while and I asked Mom if it was true."

Neil laughed. "Dumb kid. You really got me in trouble, too." He turned to Randy, desperate to parlay this into a cheerful conversation. "Isn't it great being the oldest and having that kind of power?"

"Yeah," Randy said, with a loyal smile. "When Chloe was three or something, I told her our birdbath was a magic wishing well from Egypt. I said this Egyptian king gave it to me before she was born and that I could make wishes on it anytime I wanted to. For a whole week she was going out there every morning, making wishes on the birdbath. The weird thing is, most of them came true."

"Did they?" Terry asked.

Randy gave Terry an affectionate shove. "You would have been a big brother's dream."

"You guys ready for this earthshaking experiment?" David asked. He looked almost completely recovered now. He held the stone out over the pool, his hands shaking only slightly.

"Are you sure the force of that won't pull Neil in the water?" Terry asked.

Randy sighed. "A big brother's dream . . ."

David dropped the stone. Water spritzed them all. The rope began to uncoil frantically.

"Wow!" David said. "Look how deep. Look at that!"

The rope went taut, jerking Neil's ankle forward a little. "It never hit bottom!" he said. He raised his foot and moved it up and down. He could feel the rock, still suspended, on the other end.

"How long is your rope?" David asked Randy.

Randy was shining his flashlight into the water. "I thought it was about fifty feet long!"

"How could that be?" Terry asked.

Randy flicked the flashlight under his own chin, making himself look like a phantom. "Maybe this *is* the doorway to hell!" he intoned.

"Stop big-brothering me!" Terry complained.

David began hauling up wet rope, hand over hand. "This is unbelievable! Neil, please let me use the long rope! What if it's a hundred feet deep?"

"No long rope," Neil said reluctantly. He would have done almost anything to keep David occupied and happy at that point. Except risk their chance to escape. "I read an article about these pools of water in England that are so deep they can't find the bottom. They think prehistoric monsters might live in them."

"Big brothering! Big brothering!" Terry said.

"It's true!" Neil insisted.

David untied the stone. "I'll leave the rope out to dry in case we need it tomorrow."

"Put it in a circle around us," Terry said. "I heard somewhere that snakes won't crawl across rope."

"What kind of things do you guys read that you pick up all this queer information?" Randy said.

"Did you have to bring up snakes?" Neil asked Terry.

"Make a circle," Randy said. "It sounds pretty stupid, but it can't hurt."

"Maybe we should take turns sleeping," David said. "In case there's any . . . nocturnal anything that might come in here."

"Maybe we should build a fire," Terry said.

"No!" David said. "All we need is to fill up this

place with smoke. . . ." He stopped talking, turning his face away.

Neil could almost see how the memory had galloped up behind him and trampled over him. He wanted to help. "Hey—"

"It's okay. Please. You've said enough stuff to me for one night."

"No, I haven't. That's the trouble." Neil felt a sweat break out all over his body, but he ignored it. "You know what it was like when she died." His voice was low, almost a rasp. "She was a little kid. It was so horrible. Nothing else is ever going to hurt like that."

David was nodding, head down.

"If I avoided you or if I couldn't look at you or be around you for a while . . . it wasn't because I felt different about you. It was because . . ." Neil was vaguely aware of tears running down his face. "I feel the same way about you I felt about Mimi. I couldn't handle it. Having brother feelings. I just couldn't. I know it was cruel to you but . . . that's just what happened to me. I had to shut down for a while. It was all I could do. It didn't mean that I didn't . . . that I don't—"

"Okay," David said. "You don't have to—"

"But I want you to know—"

David put out his hand, even though it didn't reach all the way to Neil. He touched the space between them. "It's okay. Just . . . I can't handle all of this at once. Wait a minute." He lowered his head and took several deep breaths.

Neil glanced around. The other two were perfectly motionless, watching David. Neil realized all his muscles were tight and locked.

"I want to say something, too. Is that all right?" David asked, still keeping his head down.

"Of course," Neil said softly.

David finally looked up. "It was bad enough losing her, Neil, but it's a hundred times worse if you have guilt on top of it. All I could think about was every little minute during the fire, the different things I could have thought of, the things I could have done—"

"You couldn't—"

"I know. But that's what you think about. I know you're trying to say some of this was your fault, too, but you weren't in the house. You can't imagine, when I woke up in the hospital and they told me . . ." He turned his head away for a minute. His jaw clenched and unclenched. Then he looked back at Neil, still dry-eyed. "You don't know that feeling and you can't imagine it. And you can't help me with that. Nobody can. But—" He stopped again and looked into the middle distance. Everyone seemed to be holding their breath. "The stuff you just said to me, Neil, or tried to say . . . After she died, it was like I lost her and all the rest of you, too. I didn't have anybody. Nobody talked to me. I was as alone as you can get. I'm not whining, but it's the truth. I don't think Mom and Dad will ever really feel the same way about me again. But you . . . if you're telling me you want to be my brother

162   •

again . . . I mean really be my brother like you used to be . . ." Finally he lost it. The head went down and stayed down. His shoulders bunched together.

Randy gave Neil a significant look and moved back, out of the way. Feeling very awkward, Neil scooted over to David and rested his hand between his brother's clenched shoulder blades. "I'm sorry," Neil said. "I really am."

David covered his face with both hands. "I'll be okay in a minute."

Terry and Randy both looked politely in another direction. David rocked himself and Neil patted, as the crying wound slowly down. Neil remembered scenes like this from a time long ago. When David was finished, Neil pulled him into a quick one-armed hug and then released him.

David gave Neil a red-eyed look of gratitude, then turned and rummaged in his backpack. He took out a piece of waxed paper and blew his nose. "You guys can look at me now. I'm all right," he said to Terry and Randy.

They laughed gently, shifting positions as if that would help shift the mood.

David looked at Neil. "Can I say just one more thing?"

"Oh, god!" Terry said.

"You can say anything you want to me," Neil told him.

David smiled crookedly. "I'm sorry to be like this, Neil, but I really don't like the way Terry bandaged

163

up your hand. Would you let me wash it and wrap it up with gauze?"

Randy laughed. "Christ!" he said.

Neil knew his answer would have been different yesterday. He held out his hand.

THIRTEEN

MIDNIGHT, SATURDAY

Nobody seemed to be terribly sleepy, so they all persuaded David to open up the food rations for a snack. After all, Neil was going to rescue them right after breakfast tomorrow, so there was really a surplus of food.

They sat inside a circle of snake-repelling rope by the pool, all four flashlights propped together in the center, to make a campfire, working on Neil's Triscuits and cheddar cheese and his two apples, which Neil neatly broke in half with his hands to make four servings. His father had taught him how to break an apple. They used to share the fruit while they worked on projects together in the garage. Later, Neil had used the technique to share apples with Mimi or David. Doing it now brought back powerful longings for home.

"What are they doing right now?" Neil asked solemnly.

Everyone seemed to understand the question.

"They're probably all at somebody's house," Randy said. "Yours. Talking to cops maybe. Everybody except my dad, who won't care." As the hours in the cave had passed, Neil noticed, Randy had grown wilder looking. He had the beginnings of a noticeable black beard now and looked like a pirate with the bandanna tied around his hair.

Neil wondered how he had changed in the last twelve hours. He was dirtier, he knew that. His pristine white T-shirt was crosshatched with dirt streaks, tears, bloodstains and sweat. Not a pretty sight at all. And of course he had all his injuries bound up by Dr. David. Dirty and lame, he thought.

Terry looked older than he had this morning. His eyes had abandoned their puppy brightness and assumed a more serious expression, which was probably more like the real Terry.

Only David seemed untouched. No, that wasn't true. He was going the other way. He looked younger than he had this morning. It was partly the lingering effects of the crying, which had left him with matted eyelashes and pink cheeks, but he also had a brighter, happier light in his eyes, one Neil hadn't seen in a long time. Was it because they'd had their talk? Or maybe because, in a crisis, David just felt more alive?

Neil was lost in these observations for a minute and then realized Randy had said a pathetic thing and no one was answering him. "Your dad cares about you," Neil said. "You know that. Something like this might make him appreciate you."

"Yeah, right," said Randy.

"Are we in trouble with the police?" Terry asked. "Like is this running away or something?"

"I don't *think* so!" Randy snapped. "When we're

166

busting our asses trying to get out of here. Nobody better say anything like that to me!"

"God, the stuff they're all going to picture!" David said. "Car accidents, drowning, kidnapping, perverts, murder, satanic cults . . ."

"Okay!" Terry said. "We get it!"

"When are we missing persons?" Randy asked Neil. "Tomorrow morning?"

Neil finished his apple half and handed the core to David, who organized everyone's garbage, putting it in Ziplocs inside his backpack. "No. I think the missing persons rule is different for minors. God, I wish we were closer to Ormond Beach. If we were there, at least a search might work. Who's going to come out this far to look for us?"

"You're getting us out tomorrow, remember?" David said.

Neil flexed his hands. "I think I should give it a try now. That way—"

He was drowned out by a chorus of *No!*'s.

"I've climbed harder things than this," he argued. "You all seem to think this is such a big deal. When I was in Colorado—"

"You were roped to two guys who knew what they were doing," David said.

"But—"

"No! Come on. This is important and we need to be smart and do it right."

Neil slumped. "I'll be less rested tomorrow," he grumbled. "Because I'm sure as hell not going to sleep."

"We'll hit you in the head," David said.

"If something did go wrong tomorrow," Terry said, looking at Neil nervously, "what do you think the odds are of somebody finding us?"

Neil looked away from him. He felt it was a disloyal question.

"Awful," Randy said. "When they search for people, they start with places those people are known to go. They'll be screwing around with the beach and the river back home. None of us has ever said a word about caves."

"But your mom knows your cousins went to this cave," David said. "Maybe she would put two and two together."

Randy smirked. "My mother is a nice lady, David, but in her whole life I don't think she ever put two and two together."

"But the people looking for us don't have to find us," Terry said. "Somebody will explore this cave before long, won't they?"

"Maybe. Maybe not," Randy said. "It's not a known tourist attraction. And probably all the spelunkers who know what they're doing avoid this fucking asshole death trap. They probably call it some nickname, like the Devil's Revenge."

"Can we not mention the devil every five minutes?" David asked.

"We don't need to worry about being rescued," Neil said. "I can get us out."

"That's right," David said. "And we should try and get some sleep. The batteries need a rest anyway."

"Do you want us to tell you a story, Terry?" Randy teased. "Which would you like? The legend of the severed hand, or the one about the three nymphomaniacs and the rabbi?"

Terry giggled. "Neither one!"

"I want to hear that rabbi story later," David said. They laughed but no one made a move.

"Well?" Randy said. He leaned over and took his flashlight from the center, flicked it off and stretched out, bunching his backpack under his head. One by one the others followed, lying down at right angles to each other.

Terry was the last one to lie down. He curled up in a position that was almost fetal, holding his flashlight in one hand, like a weapon. David took his usual sleeping position, sprawled on his stomach like a baby, arms up around his backpack-pillow. Randy was fidgety—on his back, then on his left side, facing the others, finally on his right side, facing the wall. He was the last of the other three to fall asleep.

Neil knew all this because he was wide awake. He had no expectation of sleep.

He lay on his back with one arm under his head, looking through the crevice at the stars. His mind went to Chloe. He realized, with a sad little thrill, that she was anxious for two people tonight: her brother and him—the boy she had the hopeless crush on. Nobody would sleep tonight back home. It was worse for them because they didn't know anything. It was kind of maddening not to be able to tell them. He wondered if this was what people in jail felt like.

Maybe this was the reason prison was such a terrible punishment. What could be worse than not being able to get messages to people who love you?

Neil decided this was not a line of thought he wanted to pursue. He listened again to everyone's breathing to make sure they were all asleep. Then he flicked his flashlight on and turned it to the rock wall, carefully tracing every curve and indentation of the path he would take tomorrow, to save them.

———

Neil dreamed he had fallen into the pool and was floating slowly down, fathom by fathom, through warm indigo water. He knew he was making a mistake, being passive and not trying to swim to the top, but he felt so relaxed he kept putting off the moment when he'd have to actually kick his feet and do something.

Still, another part of his mind was warning him that the deeper he let himself fall, the farther he was getting from the surface. Air was no problem. He was comfortably breathing water. He could actually feel, in the dream, the warm liquid going in and out of his lungs. It was a delicious sensation.

He squinted through the murky water and realized there were signposts at various depths. They were the names of cities. Macon, Atlanta, Chattanooga, Lexington. *I'm falling north!* he mused. Then something told him that if he fell as far as Cincinnati, he would never be able to turn back. Cincinnati was his mother's hometown. He'd been there a few times to visit his grandparents.

170

He began to worry, now, and thrashed his arms and legs, trying to get some upward momentum before that Cincinnati signpost came into view. He knew if he got there, he would just disappear, pop out of existence. He struggled hard, but the water had a current, a downward pull. His dream mind panicked.

Then he realized his pockets were full of rocks. This was the trouble! Frantically he jammed his hands into the tight jeans pockets, working out handfuls of pebbles and tossing them away, as he continued to kick with his feet. Below him now, he could see the next murky signpost coming up and he knew what it was.

In desperation, he stripped his jeans off and kicked them away. His body reversed itself like a rocket and shot up through the water, breaking the surface. . . .

Neil opened his eyes and saw the familiar ironing-board window to the night sky. *Shit, what a stupid dream!* He listened to the steady drip of stalactite water, comforting as the tick of a bedroom clock, until he felt calmer.

He groped for his flashlight, turned it on and looked at his watch. Two-thirty. He used his light to scan the whole chamber, probing into corners for lurking nocturnal monsters. Nothing scuttled. Good.

Then he scanned his companions. All sleeping soundly, the bastards. Terry actually had the effrontery to snore softly. Randy was all clenched up, having his own bad dreams, it looked like. Neil didn't know whether to wake him or not. David had scooted closer to Neil and was now up in a parallel line with him, the way they slept in the twin beds at home. In sleep, as always, David's face was angelic and peaceful. He bore a painful, powerful resemblance to Mimi.

Neil went over his climbing route one more time, thinking about how many coaches had warned him of his tendency to overtrain. There were two dangerous areas on the course. About halfway up the calcite there was a big, smooth bump that he had to either step around or climb over. It was large and round and offered poor handholds. It was a place to slow down, change the pace and be extra careful. It came at a place where he'd be tempted to speed up. So it was good to rehearse. That pitfall wasn't going to get him.

Then there was that really nasty place, higher up, when he would have to swing out and dangle. Neil didn't like that at all. One wrong grip right there and it was curtains. Pressed up against rock, you could lose your balance again and again, because if you noticed it quickly enough, your muscles could hug the rock until you stabilized. But as you hung in the air, it was all up to the hands. One slip, you'd panic and you'd drop. And from that height a guy didn't want to fall. This was a psychological course, a test in staying calm and not choking. The trouble was, Neil sometimes did lose it when the pressure was high. A standard strategy he and Randy employed in basketball was that Neil did the shooting early when he was relaxed and Randy was not fully alert, but when the pressure was high in the last few minutes, always pass to Randy. Neil was prone to some horrific mistakes when a lot was at stake. Other people's expectations gave him tremors all over.

So you know all this. So you're prepared. You won't let that happen. You can force yourself to be calm if calm is what it takes. You have to.

If he got past that place, the rest was cake. Beautiful ledges and holds all the way to the ceiling. No problem with the heights. Neil loved heights, was not afraid of them at all.

That thought made him realize he hadn't felt claustrophobic in hours. Was that because this chamber was bigger or had this horrible experience simply cured him?

Just for good measure, Neil ran the course with his light one more time. He knew it intimately now, and this time, the routine of it made him feel a little sleepy. He switched off the light and lay back, listening to Randy's fitful, muffled little sounds until he fell asleep again.

———

Neil opened his eyes because someone was shining a light into them. "What is it?" he muttered irritably.

But when he sat up, he saw the other three were still sleeping. Then the beam of light passed over him again. Neil looked up to the ceiling crevice just in time to catch the edge of the light sweeping by. "Anybody down there?" called a man's voice. It sounded like Neil's father!

Neil jumped up, a literal jump, a basketball jump. "Yes! We're here! *Help!*" he screamed. He looked frantically down at the others, who still lay motionless. "You guys! Somebody's out there! Wake up!"

"It sounds like there's somebody in there." Another man's voice. Terry's father?

"Yes!" Neil screamed. "Yes! We're here! We're all here! *Help!*"

None of the other boys was moving. What the hell was wrong with them? Losing his temper, Neil kicked David lightly in the ribs. "Hey!"

David's body jerked, but he continued to sleep.

"Hey!" Neil's voice grew soft, panicky.

"Nobody could survive down there." Someone else's voice. It was Mr. Isaacson. "There's really no point in looking."

Neil looked up, a cold sweat running into his eyes. He could see the edge of a pair of Hush Puppies at the crevice. His dad's shoes. "Dad! Look down here! Can't you hear me? Why can I hear you if you can't hear me? I'm here! I'm alive, even if . . ."

He looked down again at the other boys. He could see it now. The pallor, the stiffness. Their faces were like carved marble. A fork of grief stabbed into his stomach. Then he felt enraged. He knelt by Terry, grabbing him by the shoulders and roughly pulling him up. "Wake up!" Neil growled. He lost it and shook Terry violently. Terry's head lolled back. Neil's fingers felt as if they were gripping frozen meat. He let go in revulsion.

Crawling on his hands and knees, he went to Randy and pounded him with his fist. "Wake up! Wake up, you son of a bitch!" Randy flopped around like a rag doll. "Damn you!" Neil growled.

174

Panting now, Neil turned to David. He took his brother by the shirtfront and pulled him into a sitting position. David's head snapped back. "Not you," Neil begged, tears coming up through the anger now. "Please. Not you." Waves of sorrow shook him. He pulled David into his arms, but it was like holding an iron doorstop. "Not again," Neil sobbed.

"Let's face it, Will," Randy's father said. "Nobody could be trapped here this long and survive. We all have to get on with our lives."

"No!" Neil cried, dropping David and standing up again. "No! I'm still alive! Don't give up on me!"

"My boys are very resourceful," his father was saying. "I think they could survive a long time if they had to."

"Some son of a bitch is going to pay for this, that's all I know." This was Mr. Quinn again.

"Will," said Randy's father gently. "Let's go home. You're tired. Your wife needs you. Let's give it a rest."

"No, you've found me! I'm here!" Neil shrieked. "Don't leave me in here with . . . them!" He glanced down and thought their thin, stiff arms already looked like bones. "Please, Daddy! I'm here! Come find me! *Please!*" And then he was crying too hard to scream anymore. He heard the men walking away. A car started up in the distance. "DAAAAAAAADDY!"

A warm pair of arms circled him, half hugging, half muzzling him. Neil's face was pressed against a cotton tank top. David's. David was alive. David was trying to wake him up from this fucking nightmare. "Shut up, man," David whispered. "Daddy's not here."

175

Neil pretended to still be half-asleep while he recovered from the embarrassment. It also let him hold on for a second. Then he said, "Oh, jeez" and pushed his brother away, glancing at Randy and Terry, grateful they were still asleep, or pretending to be.

"What did I do?" Neil wiped his face with the back of his hand, casually removing tears. "What did I say?"

"Just 'Daddy, Daddy!' I don't think they heard anything."

Neil tried to force his breathing to slow down. "I dreamed you were dead," he blurted and then wished he hadn't said it.

"No such luck," David said, smiling. "You're still stuck with me."

"It was horrible." Neil shook himself as if pieces of the dream were clinging to him. "It was unusually horrible."

David rested his hand on Neil's shoulder. "It wasn't real. Everything's going to be all right. Tomorrow night at this time you'll be back home in bed dreaming about nymphomaniacs and rabbis, just like a normal guy."

"Yeah, right. Even if things go right tomorrow, I'll have nightmares about this little episode for the rest of my life."

"No kidding. But right now, you should try and go back to sleep. We're all counting on you and you need your rest."

"Yeah."

David's hand was still touching his shoulder. Neil covered it with his own for a few seconds, then pulled away and lay down again. He felt like anything but sleep. His heart was still racing and he was chilled from sweating in this cold, dark place. His head throbbed with pain.

"See up there?" David said softly. His finger was pointing to the hole in the ceiling. "Cygnus?"

Neil looked up, studying the partial pattern of stars. "Yeah."

"Remember Dad teaching us all the constellations? On that camping trip?"

"Yeah."

"That was cool. I'll never forget any of them."

Neil's heart was slowing down. "Me neither."

"Sometime we should go to the planetarium," David whispered. "Or is that a nerdy thing to do?"

"No," Neil said. "That would be cool. Maybe we'll all go."

There were sounds of David shifting into a different position, preparing to sleep again. "Good. See you in the morning."

"Okay." Neil sighed involuntarily and resettled his body. He almost felt as if he could sleep now.

His last conscious thought was that God might have picked the wrong one of them to be the older brother.

FOURTEEN

8:00 A.M., SUNDAY

Neil opened his eyes and winced. A dazzling light danced in the air around him. His body was stiff and cold, his left knee and right hand throbbed with pain. He heard water splashing nearby.

Slowly he sat up, covering his face with his hands, digging his fingers into the roots of his hair. He tried to assemble reality in his mind. There was just the slightest chance, he felt, that the whole cave thing had been a nightmare itself and if he took his hands away from his face just right, he'd see his bedroom window with the sun shining on the privet hedge outside. The splashing could be David, taking an enthusiastic shower. The musty smell could be the laundry hamper. . . .

The splashing stopped and David called out, in an unmistakably cave-resonated voice. "Are you all right?"

Neil took his hands away. The death trap, he had to admit, was especially pretty this morning. The sun streamed in from the skylight and struck the agitated surface of the pool, which cast fluttering reflections on the white calcite walls. The effect was like hundreds of pairs of wings.

David, to Neil's horror, was skinny-dipping in the bottomless-doorway-to-hell pool. He had propped his arms over the side to talk to Neil, as casually as if he were at a backyard barbecue. Neil also noticed that Terry was missing and Randy was still asleep, crumpled and scowling.

"Get your irresponsible ass out of that water!" Neil yelled, crawling over to the pool. "Now!"

"I'm being careful!" David snapped. He always got huffy when scolded. "Unlike everyone else here, I have some standards about personal hygiene."

Neil grabbed a handful of his brother's wet hair and yanked it, providing a strong incentive for David to pull himself up out of the water or suffer root damage. "I have some standards about not letting you guys get killed before we can get out of here! Come on!" He gave the hair another sharp tug, just to hurry David up.

"Okay! Okay!" David hauled it up and out, smacking Neil's hand away. "Shit! That hurt!" On purpose, he shook his head violently, showering Neil with cold water. "Give me something to dry off with so I don't get muddy."

Neil frowned at him one more time and then looked around. Terry had left David's diving jacket behind, scrunched up as if he'd used it for a pillow last night. Neil picked it up, shook it out and tossed it to his brother, just hard enough that David had to swing off balance a little to catch it.

David stood up, teetering on the rocks that edged the pool. He briskly toweled down his narrow body with the jacket. "You got up on the wrong side of the bed," he grumbled.

"I'm mad at you! That was a stupid thing to be doing, especially when nobody was watching you!"

"I'm a lifeguard, remember? This is my element." David bent down, scooped up a handful of his element and pitched it in Neil's face.

Neil shook his head like a dog. "If you're a lifeguard, you know all about swimming in places you don't know, where any kind of current or whirlpool might—"

"Keep it down!" Randy growled, shifting around. "People are trying to have nightmares over here!"

Neil laughed and turned back to David. "Where's Terry?"

David pulled up his cutoffs and zipped them. "Reading room. I think he went there because of what I was doing. He has this big thing about privacy and naked people."

Neil's filthy, sweaty T-shirt was now a rag. He pulled it apart, rather than taking it off. He felt as if he had layers of dirt on himself. He filled his canteen in the pool and poured the cold water over his head and upper body, leaning out over the water. "Yeah. What's his problem, anyway? What does he do in PE? Jeez! This is freezing! How did you put your whole body in here?"

"Mind over matter," David shrugged. He tied his shoes and knelt by his backpack, unzipping it. "Terry doesn't take PE. He's got asthma."

Randy was sitting up now, looking grumpy. "Watch David take out a shaving kit and a three-piece suit," he muttered. He crawled over to the pool on all fours and dipped one hand in the water, snatching it back as if scorched: "Shit! You two must have Viking blood. Now I have to decide whether I want to stink or freeze to death!"

"I'll help you decide." Neil upturned a canteen over Randy's head.

Randy reacted with an animal snarl and some kind of flurry of arms and legs. "You—" he shrieked. He stuck both arms in the pool and splashed Neil with a double handful. Water went up Neil's nose and into his lungs. He coughed violently.

Neil was delighted. He hadn't felt anywhere near playful for twenty-four hours. He splashed Randy back and they gave themselves up to a small water war, gritting their teeth and laughing at the same time. It was an effective way to get clean.

When they were both thoroughly wet, the momentum wound down and they shared David's damp jacket, drying off their faces. Then Neil turned to David, who was sitting back on his heels, waiting patiently for their attention. He had arranged what was left of their food in a neat pile a safe distance from all the flying water. "I thought we should see what we have left," he said. "It looks like Terry's the only one we didn't plunder."

Randy retied his bandanna and dug into his hip pocket. He pulled out his snake rattle and flourished it. "Still in good shape," he said happily.

Neil cringed at the soft, dry echo. "Don't," he said.

181

"Here's what we have left," David continued patiently. "Three peanut butter and jelly sandwiches, a bag of Cheez Doodles, some celery sticks, Teddy Grahams and five boxes of apple juice."

"Every man for himself," Randy declared, snatching a box of apple juice and the bag of Cheez Doodles.

"That's not very healthy," David said.

"Neither is rotting away in a stinking cave!" Randy retorted. He stuffed a big handful into his mouth.

Neil was repulsed by all the food options. "Just some juice, waiter," he said.

"You're not climbing rocks on an empty stomach." David handed him a drink box and one of Terry's sandwiches, which looked as if a car had run over it. "Why don't you have some celery, too?" David urged.

Neil opened his sandwich and peered inside. "You'll be lucky if I eat this piece of shit thing. Don't try to push vegetables on me at seven in the morning. Anyway, celery gives me gas."

Randy snickered, as he always did at the mention of any bodily function. "We don't want him up there climbing rocks and farting!" he said to David. "He might start an avalanche!"

They were all giggling when Terry came back. "Neil, you're weird," he said. He came and knelt in the circle, sizing up the food. He had fuzz on his chin now, which only made him look cuter and younger, like a baby animal. "That Baudelaire is the weirdest stuff I ever read!"

"You were in there long enough to read the whole thing," David said, handing him a sandwich.

"There was this one poem where it sounded like

this guy was kissing dead people or something!" Terry put the sandwich down and edged closer to Randy, looking hopefully at the Cheez Doodles bag. "Those are technically mine," he said.

"You have a choice," Randy said. "They're either mine now, or they're ours."

"Ours." Terry plopped down beside him. Randy put the bag between them.

"None of you guys are thinking about your health or your strength!" David complained. He forced an apple juice box into Terry's hand. "At least drink that!"

Terry set the drink aside and turned back to Neil. "Why would you ever want to read such horrible stuff?"

Neil shook his head. "I don't know. It seems like that was a long time ago." He gave his sandwich back to David, who was forcing down some celery to prove his point. "I really can't eat this. Let me try the Teddy Grahams." His stomach felt a little jumpy, to tell the truth. He was already thinking about the task ahead. He ate a few handfuls very quickly, then felt a sharp cramp in his stomach. *Great,* he thought. *I'll probably be fifty feet in the air and have an attack of the shits.*

When they were done, David packed up the leftovers, which everyone looked at in a kind of heavy silence. Neil thought they were realizing all at once that now there wasn't enough for another meal.

"I have to go to the bathroom," Neil said abruptly. He did have to, but mostly he just wanted to get away from everyone for a minute.

He took a leak and then absently picked up Baudelaire, which now had a fair number of pages missing. Once, when the poetry book was all he had, he would open it at random and let it speak to him like an oracle. He did it now. The poem was "The Enemy." Neil knew it by heart but read it over anyway.

Now I have reached the autumn of my mind,
I must with spade and rake turn gardener,
Restore again the inundated ground,
Where water hollows holes like sepulchres.

Neil put the book down. That seemed like a good place to stop. Forever.

Neil washed his hands in the spring and took a long drink of cold water. He jogged in place and did a few leg stretches. He felt very calm. He turned and walked back.

The others were already standing by, holding ropes and gloves for him, looking expectant. David had coiled up the rope and secured it neatly. "You want this over your shoulder? Or do you want to snap the hook on your belt?"

Neil pictured it several ways. "Clip it on the back belt loop for me. I don't care if it hits me in the butt but I don't want it interfering with my arms and legs."

David clipped it on. Just for a second, Neil thought of a dog being leashed. "How's your hand and your knee?" David asked.

Neil had forgotten them. Now suddenly they both hurt. "Not a problem!" he flared.

Randy stepped in, patting Neil on the arm. "Now look. No showing off, okay? Just get up and get yourself out. Right?"

Neil immediately felt better. "I might want to do a little ballet or collect some rock samples."

Terry tipped his head back, turning his face into the sunbeams. "It makes me dizzy just to look up there!"

Everyone glared at him.

"Where are you going to start from?" David asked.

Neil led them to the calcite formation he liked best. It was very ridgy and bumpy and gave him a multitude of options while he was getting his bearings. He scanned it, making sure it seemed the same up close, chose a handhold and started up, propping a shoe on the slippery surface, finding traction, pulling up with his arm, letting his other foot leave the ground and find its own traction spot, looking up and reaching again.

His body registered delight. Climbing was its favorite thing. He felt an eagerness in his muscles and he gave in to it, letting his arms pull and his legs intuitively search for the best purchase. His first worry was that the calcite would be so slick his feet would be slipping all around, but the rubber soles were grabbing it nicely. Out of sheer joy, he quickly mounted to a height of about twenty feet and then paused and glanced down at his audience.

"Nice job!" Randy said, clapping. "Keep going, baby!" This was basketball court talk, very effective. Neil's mind bloomed with pleasant memories: the squeak of his high-tops on a polished wood floor, his legs pounding downcourt, his fingertips magically projecting the ball into the hoop. People yelling and cheering for him—total strangers! The peripheral glances at cheerleaders jumping up and down, their shiny legs flashing between the thick white socks and the little short skirts. The most erotic image in the world to Neil was cheerleaders' legs. They were shinier and more beautifully turned than the legs of any other kind of women. Randy had brought back all that nice imagery with one catch phrase.

Now Neil was remembering the athlete in himself, the champion. His body itched for achievement and conquest. He scaled calcite faster, heart pounding, breathing deep and fast. At a height of about fifty feet he paused again. The boys below were starting to look smaller.

"Quit looking down!" David shouted.

"I like to look down!" Neil argued. "I love to look down!"

"They say you're not supposed to look down!" David complained to the others.

"Let him alone! He's the one doing it!" Randy said. He clapped again, as if he wanted to drown David out. "Come on, Neil. You're looking great."

Neil decided he needed to tune them both out at this point. He didn't need fear or confidence. He needed to start paying attention as the course got rougher. The fun part was over.

He collected his thoughts. He was now about ten feet from what he had targeted as the first major obstacle on the course—a huge round slope of calcite that he had to cross in order to reach the next level. He would have to hug it and ease around it with his whole body. It should work, he thought, because his traction was better than he'd expected. His shoes gripped the calcite well, and he was using his bare hands for this part of the climb, so he could sense any slippage the second it happened. His injuries weren't causing too much trouble. His hand hurt more than his knee, but both were doing their work without too much pain. There were a couple of minor annoyances. The rope swinging against his ass was an irritating distraction. He would forget it was there and it would swat and surprise him, making a jump in his concentration.

And that was the real problem. He didn't think his concentration was all that good. On other climbs he had had a different feeling, a highly alert, aware mind. Now he felt sort of giddy and high. Looking back over where he'd been, he realized some of it had been almost unconsciously climbed. He couldn't actually remember the moment-to-moment sequence. None of this was good. He knew he needed sobriety in case an emergency happened. He couldn't afford a sense of rapture.

Still, he wanted more than anything to look down again. This was special. This climb would happen only once and he wanted to see it and remember it. He decided that if maybe he indulged himself really well, he could settle down and get on with things.

Moving carefully, he crossed his feet and flipped himself around quickly, leaning back and hugging the wall with his arm and shoulder muscles, but now facing out toward The Chamber. The spectacle was overwhelming, like looking at a cathedral from high in the balcony.

"What are you *doing*?" David screamed.

"Sight-seeing!" Neil called back. He estimated he was between sixty and seventy feet in the air. In front of him, sunbeams slanted down, loaded with dancing, sparkly debris. Like spotlights, they struck the surface of the pool, making amberish circles on its surface. From this height, the pool water was such a dark blue it appeared almost black. The little stream looked artificial, small and metallic. The calcite ballooning around him was not the uniform white it appeared from a distance. It was a cream color, streaked with yellow and pink. Again, Neil thought of ice cream. The walls all around at his eye level seemed alive, stalactites dripping water, mica glittering in the limestone ledges. The watery sounds were richer up here, more melodious. Neil thought he could hear the echoes of his own breath.

Looking higher, he felt a jolt at seeing the sky so much closer, maybe only thirty feet away. That was his life out there, his freedom. He knew he could reach it. The sun was climbing in the sky now, beating on his face, making him perspire.

One of his sneakers slid, catching him off guard. Adrenaline surged. His muscles instinctively gripped backward but he was in the wrong position to really grab on. That fucking rope was now a barrier.

Involuntary gasps and cries bubbled up from below. Sweat trickled into Neil's left eye, burning. *Think.* He raised his arm tentatively to try to turn himself the right way. His change of balance made his foot slide a few more inches. He froze, waiting for his balance to stabilize.

"You turn your ass around the right way *now* and quit horsing around!" David's voice was shrill.

"He doesn't need you to tell him that, asshole!" Randy countered. "Just stay calm, Neil. You're all right. Go slow."

Neil began to appreciate Terry. He might have his head up his ass half the time, but he knew when to keep his mouth shut, too.

The only thing Neil knew for sure was that he couldn't hold on to these rocks with his back forever. So he had to turn around and risk it. Inching his head around, he looked up for a solid handhold somewhere above and to the left. There was one. He inhaled sharply, swung his right arm and let his body flip. His hand gripped the rock securely, but his feet slid wildly, causing a chorus of terrified squeaks from below. Neil thought they sounded like a bunch of hamsters. "Relax!" he called. He knew he was fine. His handhold was secure and he waited for his body to calm down, then carefully reset his feet. He exhaled. "And could you guys please shut up with the advice? I'm not going to die on purpose or anything!"

"We can't tell that from here!" David shot back. "You just do it straight from now on and quit acting up, all right?"

Neil couldn't agree more. He waited until his breathing was completely calm and edged over to that big bump. In a different mood, he might have tried a lighthearted, fast maneuver across it, but he thought he'd used enough of his luck for one day. He threw his left leg over the hill of rock and straddled it obscenely, casting blindly on the other side for a new handgrip.

This posture, of course, brought a new chorus of yells from below.

"Ride her, baby! Give her one for me!"

"You don't have time for that, Neil. Get back to climbing!"

"She's better looking than most of his girlfriends."

At least they weren't afraid anymore. Neil found his hold and slowly dragged his right leg over the rock.

Randy made an obscene groan. "Was that good for you, Neil? It was really good for us."

"Shut up!" Neil laughed uneasily. Suddenly his right hand was giving him trouble. It felt as if it was swelling under the bandage, pounding with every heartbeat. Sweat was pouring into his eyes. He should have thought to borrow the bandanna. He wasn't having fun anymore.

And now, here was the hardest part of the whole climb. The transition from calcite to limestone, where he had to swing out and hang. He decided to try to control the spectators first.

"I'm going to do something in a minute that will look scary," he called down. "But it's not. Anybody who's right under me should move back."

"Why?" David cried.

"Because I said so!"

Silence below. Neil studied his objective, a beautiful, wide ledge of limestone above his head, just inside his reach and to the left. Above it, a virtual ladder all the way to the ceiling. Below it, no footholds at all. A smooth wall. *This is all psychological. Just rehearse it and do it.*

He had to grab it with his good left hand, then let go with his feet and swing out, grabbing on with his right hand and letting his feet dangle until he could get them to find a purchase on the smooth wall and walk him up there. It was a nice, wide ledge. No reason for it not to work. The problem, like the problem of jumping off a high dive, was just making your body do something it resisted.

He tried to psych himself with the objective. He looked up at the sky again. That beautiful blue sky. He thought maybe he felt a breeze. *Geronimo,* he thought and out went the hand.

Circuits jammed. Adrenaline hissed and fizzed in his blood. His body acted, a swift series of movements, before he could even think what had happened. Seconds later, amid the screams from below, Neil sorted the event in his brain.

His good hand had grabbed a chunk of soft, crumbling, worthless rock, mushy as mud. It gave way, scattering pebbles and shards like fairy dust down on the boys below. Since Neil was basically flying through the air at the time, his right hand had gone on with its orders, grabbing the other end of the ledge, which, thankfully, was solid and holding.

But here was the problem. Neil Gray, a 192-pound boy, was hanging from a questionable ledge by the fingers of one injured hand. The rest of his body was worthless weight, dangling like a mobile in space. He knew how bad this was by how numb he felt. He was dazed. His heart and blood were sending in no reports. The cave seemed very quiet.

"It's okay," he called down in a pathetically frightened voice. "Don't be scared."

No response to this piece of nonsense. Not even a hamster squeak.

Try anything. Even though he knew it wouldn't work, Neil tried to reach up with his good arm. But his fingers fell inches short of the ledge. Neil swung himself a little, trying to find the wall with his feet. Nothing, plus the movement loosened his finger grip a little. Next he tried flexing his right arm to see if he could pull his whole body up by sheer grit. The muscles of his arm ground together impotently until they got tired and gave up. A new layer of sweat broke over the old one. Those were the only things he could think of to do and he couldn't do them!

Neil ventured a look down. His friends and brother looked very distant, very small.

His right hand began to send urgent pain signals. He knew his fingers were going to betray him any minute and let go. He knew it. Where was that fucking superhuman strength people were supposed to call on in times like these?

Down below, he heard some kind of involuntary whine or sob. David.

"Shut him up!" Neil roared so loudly it made his body swing like a puppet. His hand slid a little further on the rocks.

David's sound stopped abruptly. Everything was very silent and almost peaceful for a second. Neil had one more idea. He thought maybe he could just try to double at the waist and swing his feet up wild, hoping they could grab or hit the ledge. It was a long shot. But if he tried that and fell, he'd be falling head-first and break his neck. The way he was now, he would fall straight down and maybe only injure his lower body.

He realized with a wave of despair that was the only choice he had in the matter. How he would fall. "Get back," he called in a broken voice, and he felt his fingers unclench and the wind rush up his nose.

FIFTEEN

At first, falling was so beautiful it permitted none of the appropriate bad feelings. For just a second, it was the same as some of Neil's best flying dreams. The ground was so far away. Neil felt a supreme rush of freedom, even though he knew the ground was about to assert itself and suck him back into the prison of gravity. A painful, mangled death would almost be worth it, he felt, for a moment of airborne bliss like this.

Then there was despair. *This is not a dream. Nothing in the world can stop you from hitting the ground.*

Then the scenery, which had been gliding past him slowly, suddenly speeded up in a tremendous rush, and Neil felt a kind of abandon. *If I'm dead, I'm dead.*

He heard three sounds. One was like pudding hitting a sidewalk. Another was a sickening *crack*, like the leg breaking off a piece of furniture. Simultaneously the other three boys had all made a kind of grunting sound, as if they'd smacked into something themselves.

Then stillness. Then the pain.

Neil had been injured many times in his life. Ordinary sports injuries, a broken arm when he was in sixth grade, his appendix out when he turned sixteen. He'd never felt pain like this. This pain, which he vaguely located in his lower body, was like a voice screaming at him. *Do something!* It was such an insistent, shrewish pain, it made him angry. It wanted him to look and he didn't want to look.

Drenched in cold sweat, dizzy and nauseated, he turned his face in the direction of the scream. It was his right leg, not just broken but shattered. His right foot, for instance, was turned the wrong way and the whole angle of the leg was wrong, like a child's drawing. He prayed that under his jeans there were no bones poking out through the skin. He'd seen that once in his father's office and he never wanted to see it again. This was grotesque enough, comic almost. Another wave of nausea hit him and he held his breath to avoid vomiting.

He gradually became aware that the other three boys were closing in on him, creeping up slowly, as if the injury might have made him dangerous. Neil hardly noticed them because there were so many voices arguing in his mind. *There's no way for you to get out of here now. You let everyone down. This is a relief. Now no one can expect anything more of you.*

David knelt beside Neil, trembling so hard his hair shook. He and Neil stared crazily into each other's eyes for a second, sharing the horror. "Try to move the toes on your *left* foot," David croaked.

195

At first this seemed irrational, but Neil saw that David was way ahead of him. The right leg was obviously wrecked. David was checking for something worse, like spinal damage.

Spinal damage! Neil clenched and released the toes of his left foot rather frantically. Even through his sneaker the movement was obvious. He and David sighed with relief.

"Maybe it's just the one leg," David said.

Neil began to flex things—his arms, his neck, his back—just to be sure. Vainly he sent a message to his right foot and got no response at all. "That's what it seems like."

"I'm going to try to touch it," David warned. Slowly and carefully he untied Neil's right shoe and eased it off. Neil whined involuntarily, the sound a dog might make on a stormy night.

Terry leaned in. "Does it hurt?"

Randy and David both whirled on Terry. Terry stepped back and shut up.

David turned back to Neil. "This ankle must be broken clean through for your foot to be going that way. We really need to get your pants off and see what everything else looks like."

Neil held up a weak hand. "Wait, though. Just give me a minute." He had to lie back in the dirt. He felt so dizzy. Immediately that fucking hole in the ceiling came into view. Without warning, Neil began to cry. "I'm sorry," he wailed. "I *tried.*"

Randy moved in, tucking David's jacket under Neil's head. "You were doing great," he said. "Nobody could have known that rock would be soft. You did more than any of us could have done. We're just glad you're alive."

"But what are we going to do?" Neil's voice was a six-year-old's now.

"First we're going to deal with fixing you," David said. "I have to figure out some way to set your leg. Every time you move, you could do more damage to yourself."

Neil closed his eyes. The sky was making him sick. "What difference does it make?" he whimpered. The pain was a part of his bloodstream now, jangling like caffeine. His blood felt hot and jumpy. Little tremors were running up and down his arms. Now he understood what people meant when they said they had pain so bad it made them want to die.

"Maybe I can take the handle off the shovel and splint you that way," David was saying.

"Do you know what you're doing?" Randy asked. "You don't want to do something that would hurt him worse."

"There's nothing worse than broken bones rattling around loose," David said. "They could puncture his skin or get way out of place. Even if I set it so it heals wrong, it's better than no set at all. I'm pretty sure I can do it in a temporary way. I've seen Dad do it a million times. Go get the shovel from the bathroom."

Neil closed his eyes. The pain was following his pulse now, making his body feel like the light on top of a police car. "Why are you wasting your time?" he whispered to David. "Give it up. I'm never getting out of here alive and you know it. Think about getting yourselves out."

"Oh please. What movie is that from?"

"It's true."

Terry's voice. "How are we going to get out now? That was our last chance!"

David's voice changed directions, turning toward Terry. "Keep quiet! You're not injured. So if you piss me off, I can smack you one. And when Neil's all better, I'm going to smack him one, too. Just about the last thing we need right now is either one of you saying a bunch of negative crap."

Neil sighed. There was something ironic in this, since they'd been picking on David for being negative through the whole ordeal. Neil felt very tired. The pain was sapping him. He hoped he was falling asleep or passing out. Then he wondered if he might be bleeding internally. He decided not to mention it.

Randy was back. "The head of the shovel screws on. So you're in business if we can find something to use for a screwdriver. I'm sure you've got something in your magic bag that will work."

"Somebody give me a dime," David said.

Neil was losing interest. He thought about Chloe. There was some song he was remembering about a girl who died just as she was about to tell the boy next door she loved him. It was always, he realized, the girls who died in the songs. He wondered if Chloe would put flowers on his grave. *Do you even get a grave if there's no body?* Do they bury an empty coffin? He realized he was being unzipped. "Hey!" he grumbled, opening his eyes. "Let me die with dignity."

"You always were a complete piece of shit when you were sick," David said. "Brace yourself." Gently and carefully, he edged Neil's jeans down over his hips. Every little jostle was a new and different knife at a new and different angle. Neil cried out.

"Shit!" David said. "Maybe I should have cut these off you."

"I want a real doctor!" Neil said.

Inch by painful inch, David got Neil's jeans off him. Randy hovered attentively. Terry had moved out of Neil's line of vision. When the entire leg was exposed, Randy and David gazed at it in horror.

"Jeez!" Randy said.

Even though he felt drained and hopeless, Neil was still curious enough to lift his head and see what was so scary. No greenstick fractures, but it still wasn't very pretty. His leg was swollen and beginning to turn a variety of colors. There was a bloody scrape all along the calf. His knee looked wrong somehow, in the wrong place or at the wrong angle. And his shin bone was slightly turned, accounting for the ninety-degree foot angle.

"Damn it!" David remarked. Still, he plunged right in, putting one hand under Neil's misshapen foot and lifting carefully. He made a quarter turn, watching Neil's face for reaction.

The pain shrieked up Neil's body all the way to his head. "No!" he shouted.

"I'm sorry," David said, but continued rotating until Neil's foot went the right way.

Neil panted from pain. "Give me something. Don't you have anything in the first aid kit?"

David shook his head. "I'm sorry. It should feel better in a minute."

"It doesn't feel better!" Neil noticed that Randy was holding his hand. He wasn't sure when that had happened. He noticed it now because Randy squeezed. Neil squeezed back. "I'm sorry. It really hurts."

"I know." David was studying Neil, scanning his face, then his leg, then his face again. "I need to push this shin bone in a little, okay?"

Neil closed his eyes. "Okay," he whispered.

Randy gripped a little tighter. "Keep your eyes closed," he suggested.

But Neil had to look. David touched Neil's calf several times, like a golfer addressing the ball. Then he pressed in gently on the shin bone. Something audibly popped into place. Neil's leg looked like a leg again. A battered, swollen, broken leg, but definitely a real leg. Pain signals exploded like fireworks in Neil's brain. He went limp and a few sobs bubbled up out of him involuntarily.

"It's okay, you're okay," Randy chanted.

Neil found himself sliding into a cavern of self-pity. "You shouldn't be wasting all this time on me," he insisted. "You should at least get yourselves out and then send help back for me. No matter what you do, I can't walk or keep up with you."

"Shut up, Neil, you're not the boss anymore," Randy said mildly. "You're on sick leave."

"But I want you guys to get out," Neil wailed. He was starting to cry again. "I want *somebody* to get out!" He turned his head to one side and sobbed.

Something flickered on that side. It was Terry kneeling down beside him. "Don't cry," Terry said, looking into Neil's face. "It scares me when I think *you're* giving up." His brown eyes were big and trusting. Neil thought of Mimi.

"I'm sorry, Terry," he sniffed. "It's just the pain. You have to ignore what I say."

"Most of the time we do that anyway," Randy told him.

Neil winced. David was pressing cold metal against his sore leg. Randy held it steady while David tied the splint in several places with pieces of gauze. Since everything had been twisted back into place, Neil had to admit that the jostling didn't hurt as much. When Randy let go of Neil's hand to help David, Terry automatically took over. His grip was warm and gentle.

When it was all over, they passed the canteen. Terry supported Neil's head so he could drink.

"Nice work, Dr. Frankenstein," Randy said to David. "It looks almost human."

"Should we cut the leg out of your jeans so you can put them back on?" David asked.

"Whatever," Neil said.

"Good," Randy said. "We're all getting an inferiority complex looking at you in your underwear."

David used his knife to saw through the denim. "I'll just make cutoffs," he said.

After all Neil had been through, a little more jostling was no trouble. He turned his head to one side and let his mind drift, as David tugged and prodded the shorts into place. "I can zip myself up!" he said, batting David's hands away. When that ordeal was over, Neil let himself go limp again. He wanted to sleep. He closed his eyes, letting the dull throb of pain lull him like a metronome.

"I'm hungry," Terry said. "What do we have left?"

"Nothing," David said. "You can't have anything. We're rationing now. We have to figure out a whole new plan."

Randy's voice. "I'm glad you think there's a new plan to figure out."

"Well . . . ," David said. "Maybe one of the three of us could climb up there."

Neil opened his eyes. "Are you crazy?"

"Yes, David, are you?" Terry said. "It won't be me, I can tell you that right now!"

"I know I couldn't do it," Randy sighed.

"Okay," David said. "Give me the rope."

"No way!" Neil said. "David, don't be an idiot. There's no way you can do that. I'm a much better climber than you and I couldn't do it. For all we know, all the limestone up there is crumbly. We can't have you breaking a leg. You're the only one who knows how to set them."

"Okay, okay," David said.

"Your only chance at this point is back out the way we came," Neil said. "I know it seemed hopeless yesterday, but it's all you have. The three of you should just make a total effort and if anyone gets out, run like hell for help for the rest of us." Neil shuddered at the thought of what he was suggesting, that they leave him here alone at the mercy of the snakes and the bats.

Randy sighed. "Even disabled, he's still going to be

the boss. But he's right, David. That's all we have. Let's get started."

"Oh, god!" Terry said.

"And we don't need any whiners either!" David snapped. "It's bad enough we don't have Neil anymore."

"Thanks for making me feel like I'm already dead."

"Don't worry," David said. "I'll kill myself before I'll let you die, you bastard! If you think I'm going to have that kind of guilt twice in one lifetime . . ." He suddenly looked beyond Neil and his eyes widened. "What is that?" he whispered.

Neil felt a jolt. For a second he had the irrational fear that David had looked beyond him and seen Mimi's ghost. He turned his head slowly in the direction David was staring and his body flinched with fright. It was such an incongruous, unexpected thing. There was a big black anhinga standing three feet from him, spreading her wings out to dry. She looked like a feathered umbrella.

"Quick. Somebody tell me you see the same thing I see," David whispered.

"It's a duck!" Terry squeaked.

"That's not a duck, you jerk!" Randy hissed. "That's—what is it, Neil?"

"It's an anhinga," Neil said softly. "But how the hell—"

"It must have flown in through the ceiling when we weren't looking," Terry said.

David's whisper was tight with excitement. Like Neil, he was obviously putting a fantastic realization together. "Like hell she did! Look at her! She's drying her wings off! Neil, tell them about anhingas! Tell them what anhingas do!"

Neil's heart pounded. "They swim underwater," he said softly. "Chinese people use them to dive for fish."

"That means she . . ." Randy looked at the pool.

"Yes!" David crept forward and squatted by the pool, peering down. "She came *in* this way! From the outside! From the outside!"

Neil felt a tear run down his face. He felt too tired to sit up and look at the pool again, so he turned his head and looked at the bird. She was gazing right at him, perhaps puzzled by his stiff leg. Neil memorized every detail of her: the glossy black feathers, the in-turned orange feet, the little shiny black eyes. She was the most important sight of his whole life.

Terry approached the pool now. "Do you mean . . ."

"All this time," David said. "We've been sitting here by the door!"

"Oh, god!" said Randy. "Do you think we can really get out that way?"

"Well, sure," David said uncertainly. "If she can hold her breath long enough to get in, we can hold our breaths long enough to get out. If she jumps back in the water, we could just follow her. She'd show us the way."

Randy was blushing, something Neil had never seen him do. "I guess this would be a good time to mention I can't swim."

"Oh, god, that's right," Neil said.

"How can you get to be seventeen and not know how to swim?" David asked impatiently.

Randy shrugged. "Until I moved here and met Neil, I didn't even know I could do athletic stuff. I had a very deprived childhood. They kept focusing on my brilliant mind."

Terry elbowed Randy gently. "When you come right down to it, you're a nerd, just like me."

"Think again, Cookie Boy! You want to see what I can do in a fistfight?"

Terry was still laughing. "It's not just you," he said. "I don't know if I can swim underwater very well, either. I mean, holding my breath is not a good thing for me."

"And I have a piece of metal strapped to my leg," Neil pointed out.

"It's still okay," David said. "I can tow you, all of you. We'll just go one person at a time. All you guys have to do is hold your breath and not suck water and drown for a couple of minutes. Can everyone do that?"

"You'll be like the ferryboat guy at the gates of hell," Randy said.

"Here we go talking about hell again!" Terry complained.

"I can do it," David insisted.

"Yeah, you and Neil can do everything," Randy said. "Neil can walk up walls like a fly and you can swim the English Channel. I think the best thing, David, is for you to just swim out of here and get help."

"No!" Neil and David said it at once.

Randy turned to Neil. "Come on! It's the sensible thing. We'll kill him making all those trips. It might be a long way to the outside. For all we know, these birds can hold their breath all day."

"He won't be able to go and leave me here," Neil said.

"Right," said David.

Randy threw up his hands. "Okay! I'm not going to try to crack the code in your crazy world. Then David can take Neil and leave us here."

"No!" Terry said.

"Oh shit!" said Randy. "Am I the only self-sacrificing one here?"

"There's me," David said. "And I can beat you with one hand tied behind my back. I'm making three trips and that's that. For all we know the outside is only two feet away."

"Or twenty miles," Neil said. "Randy's right about the bird. We don't know how long she can hold her breath. I think the best thing to do is to tie a rope to you and let you go alone and see how it is. If it's too long, we can pull you back. Then we can make the rest of the plan based on what you find out."

"The rope is only a hundred feet long," David said. "What if I need a hundred and five?"

"We'll use Randy's rope. That gives you one-fifty. If it's more than that . . . I don't know what."

"I don't need the rope. It's going to slow me down," David said. "What could go wrong anyway?"

"You could refuse to quit like you sometimes do and keep swimming until you drown. You could lose your way. A bunch of man-eating cave sharks could—"

"Okay, but . . ." David paused, because the bird had folded her wings and was waddling toward the pool. She leaned over, looking in the water. "I'm going to follow her if she dives," David said.

Neil tried to sit up. His worthless, weighted leg clanked. Pain shot up into his groin. "Don't you dare. . . ."

The bird dove headfirst. "I'm sorry," David said to Neil and dove in after her. Just a splash and he was gone. There were only three of them.

"No!" Neil shouted. "Damn you!" His body struggled to move. Pain bounced like pinballs in his leg.

"Neil, settle," Randy said. "It's too late. He's gone."

"Goddamn stupid kid! He thinks he's cute!" Neil felt a brand-new urge to cry welling up.

"Calm down!" Randy insisted. "He'll be okay. He's a champion diver. He's good at this."

"I'm good at climbing and look at me!"

Terry was just staring into the water.

"I know what you're thinking," Randy said to Neil. "But it's not going to happen. You're not going to lose him, too."

Neil had to lie back. The leg was really killing him. Tears rolled into his ears. "I won't give up another one," he said faintly.

"How long can a person hold their breath?" Terry asked the water.

"Shut up!" Randy shouted. "Can't you think about somebody besides yourself?"

"I am! I'm thinking about David!"

207

"Two minutes," Neil said to the ceiling. "Three or four if they're a good swimmer. But not much more." He closed his eyes again.

"He hates to give up!" Terry fretted. "He won't give up!"

"Shut up or I'll shut you up!" Randy said.

"Leave him alone. I'm okay," Neil said. He felt a little crazy. Pictures of Mimi's funeral were flashing in his mind. "Please," he whispered to the cave, to God, to David. The pain seemed to make him weaker and more emotional than normal. He had to lie back and close his eyes.

In a few minutes he heard their voices clamoring, heard the splash. It was almost an effort to open his eyes and look. Neil struggled up to a sitting position again.

David was stretched out flat beside the pool. His skin looked white. The other two were hovering, giving him oxygen from Terry's canister.

"Is he okay?" Neil called out.

Terry and Randy chorused. "Yeah."

Coughing, David raised his arm for Neil to see. Clenched in his fist was a dripping handful of mud and grass.

From the outside.

SIXTEEN

10:00 A.M., SUNDAY

David breathed oxygen for a good ten minutes before he was ready to sit up and tell his story. But before his lungs could recover, his eyes were already giving everything away. Neil couldn't remember the last time he'd seen such a happy eye sparkle on that kid. It told as much as the handful of turf, which was slowly disintegrating in David's clenched fist.

"Oh, god!" was David's first exclamation followed by a fit of coughing.

Randy couldn't wait any longer. He picked up David's dirty fist and shook it. "You did it, didn't you?"

David nodded, vigorous as a first-grader, still sucking on the oxygen.

Neil couldn't move, so he offered a verbal hug. "My baby brother!" he said proudly.

David's eye sparkle turned gratefully in Neil's direction.

Terry, who was administering the oxygen, refused to celebrate. "Are you going to be okay?" he fussed.

David pushed the canister away and coughed some more. "Fine, I'm . . ." (cough) ". . . fine. Okay. That's enough." (More coughing.) "I'm fine now." He took a deep breath and let it out slowly. It snagged a few times, but he was pretty much okay, Neil thought. Still, he wondered if David could manage to repeat such a grueling exercise three times. Meanwhile, though, David was wearing a shit-eating grin. "It's fabulous down there! Wait till you see it. Unbelievable. And outside! You guys . . . the light was so bright, I guess because of us being in the dark here so long, but it was blinding! It was like those guys tell about the near-death thing!"

"What a great thing to compare it to!" Randy said, rolling his eyes.

David coughed some more. "Canteen," he said to Terry. He took a long, deep drink of water. "The light was so bright outside, I could hardly see! And the water was rough out there, too. I was getting all bounced around. But I saw the fucking riverbank and I said, by god, I'm getting over there and getting my trophy and I got up on the bank so I could catch my breath and . . . you guys—"

"Catch your breath now," Neil said. "You don't have to tell us everything in one sentence."

David ignored him. "We're so far from where we went in. We're in some totally different part of the park! All the trees are different and it's—" He stopped to drink from the canteen again.

"How are we supposed to hold our breath for this little trip if you can hardly do it?" Randy asked. "And is the way clear? Can you see what you're doing? Did you follow the bird? What are the rocks like down there? Is there some way we can get trapped underwater? Because I'd rather starve up here in two weeks than suck up a ton of water in two minutes and go out like a candle!"

David was still drinking. He put the canteen down. "I only saw the bird for a second. She went too fast for me. But you can see the light in the water. There's dark water right under here and then you see a light area and you go toward it. It's very clear, no problem at all. I'll be taking you under a little rock ledge and then you're out in open water. And as for the breathing, I was swimming, so it was harder. You're just going to get towed. All you have to worry about is holding your breath and not drowning. I'm not saying it will be comfortable, but I think if it's life and death, we all can do it. It's only two and a half, maybe three minutes. And even if you do fuck up and breathe some water, I'll be right there and I know what to do. I'm telling you, I know it all sounds scary now, but when you see that surface, Randy, when you break through that surface—God! It was like something religious!"

"I'm going to keep my eyes closed the whole time," Terry said.

"Me, too," Randy said. "I don't need a religious experience."

"When we do it," David lectured, "remember to hold an inhalation, not an exhalation."

"What's the difference?" Randy asked.

"Because, if you screw up and try to breathe, you're blowing air out. If you hold an exhale, the first thing you do is suck in water. An inhale buys you a little more time."

"I'm scared," Terry said.

"I have to go to the bathroom," Randy said abruptly and walked out.

"Go to the bathroom?" David said to the others. "We're going in the water and in two minutes we'll be out of here. What's he talking about?"

"He's scared," Neil said. "He just needs a minute to pull himself together. He's more scared than Terry is. I've seen that look before. I think he's got a thing about water."

"Christ!" David said. "Every one of you guys is some kind of fucking case study."

"Not like you!" Neil said. "Look, I wouldn't mind taking a final leak myself. Frankly, in case I get scared underwater, I'd like to be all emptied out, if you get my drift. Anyway, I want to see if I can walk. Will you help me up?"

David slapped the dirt floor. "I want to get on with this thing!"

"We will. Calm down. Help me up." Neil held out his arm.

David snorted, but got up dutifully and supported Neil's weight as he stood. "Take a few steps," David said. "Just on your good leg. Don't use the bad one at all."

"I wonder how far we are from the car," Neil said. He tried a few steps, using David as his other leg. "I think I'm pretty good here." He tried to ignore the excruciating pain, which he noticed was radiating all the way into his hip joint.

"We'll get you to the fucking car," David said grimly. Three steps and he was already puffing from supporting half of Neil's weight. "We'll drag you like a dead tree if we have to. Or we'll send somebody to get the car and drive it back to you. That's what we'll do."

"Right, that's good," Neil said. "And I don't want to scare you, but our first stop is not home. It's the emergency room. I mean, you're a great doctor and all, but I have a really bad feeling I need attention for this."

"Obviously," David said. "Anyway, it's better if we call Mom and Dad from an emergency room. They can't get too mad then."

Neil laughed.

They met Randy in the doorway. He was ashen. "You started a trend," Neil said.

Randy laughed, but Neil had the feeling he hadn't even heard him. He was walking toward the pool with a zombie look on his face.

"Take Randy first," Neil whispered to David. "The longer he thinks . . ."

"Yeah," David said. "Look!" They were at the entrance to the boys' room. Randy had crossed out the word *boys* and written *men.*

"Even under stress, he's a clever guy," Neil said.

David laughed. "Do you . . . uh . . . need help or anything?"

"I sure hope not," Neil said. "Just get me to the doorway where I can lean on the wall and I think I can hold myself up with one hand. . . . I think I'm fine."

"Roger. Call me if the situation changes."

Gritting his teeth, shaking and sweating from the effort, Neil accomplished what he needed to. He felt he'd already given up enough of his dignity today without having his little brother help him go to the bathroom. When he was done, he took a final glance at Baudelaire and then called to David.

This time they crossed paths with Terry. "If everybody else is going to go . . ."

"You guys are stalling!" David exploded. "Terry, you have exactly one minute and then I'm gonna come and drag you out."

Terry scurried through the doorway.

Back at the pool, Randy was staring maniacally at the water. Neil tried to imagine what this journey would feel like to someone who had never been underwater in his life. He couldn't.

"Nice graffiti," Neil said gently.

Randy looked up. "Yeah. Speaking of which, we should write something on the wall about the pool being a way out. For the next pack of slobs that comes through here." He stood up and carefully lettered, EXIT THROUGH THE POOL. "This should never have to happen to anyone again."

David helped Neil sit down and went over to Randy. "I think I'd like to take you first, okay? Because I figure you're the easiest one."

"Oh?" Randy said.

"I'm here!" Terry said, still scurrying. "Did I miss anything?"

"Randy's going first," Neil said.

"Oh, good!" Terry said.

"Are you ready?" David touched Randy's arm.

Randy jumped. "This minute, you mean? Just like that?"

"Unless you want to pray or do a ceremony," David said. "I mean, come on! If you guys had seen the real world out there like I did—"

"Are we leaving all our stuff?" Randy said, looking around.

"Yeah," David said. "Some of the backpacks might float, but in the long run, they're going to be in my way."

"My dad'll kill me if I leave this in here!" Terry said, clutching his leather pack. "This thing cost a hundred dollars!"

"Chee!" said Randy. "Doesn't your family know about Wal-Mart?"

"I'm sorry, Terry," David said. "We're trying to survive. Anything you can put in your pocket, fine. Forget the rest."

"Good," Randy said. "Because I won't go without my rattle."

"I'm glad you're letting me take the car keys out," Neil said. "We might need those."

Terry was digging into his pockets. He pulled up the flattened, crushed wildflower he'd picked up in the woods. It was more stem than petal at this point. "This is my souvenir," he said. "It can remind me of yesterday morning, when I was young and innocent and my idea of something scary was taking a leak in the woods."

They all laughed.

"Neil, car keys don't count," David said. "You have to take something from this cave back out with you. Something that fits in your pocket."

Neil thought grimly that he was leaving parts of himself behind instead of taking things away. His poetry, his blood . . . But he wanted to humor David, so he looked around. "Can you find a piece of the rock that gave away? One of the pieces that fell down?"

David jumped up and began to look.

"What's your souvenir, David?" Terry asked.

David had found a suitable chunk of the treacherous limestone and presented it to Neil. "My souvenir is you three guys outside this cave all in one piece," David said, sliding into the pool. "Come on, Randy. Just let yourself into the water. You can hang on the side or on to me until you're ready to go."

Randy closed his eyes and took a deep breath. Then he slid, very awkwardly, into the water. He lost his grip on the side and grabbed at it frantically as his body started to sink. David pulled him up and held him until Randy grabbed on to the rocks again. Randy was trembling visibly, either from the cold or just from fear.

"Are you okay?" David asked him warily.

Randy nodded.

"I'll show you how I'm going to hold you," David said, treading water in Randy's direction. "Please don't get startled and hit me."

Randy laughed a terrorized laugh. "I won't."

Moving very slowly, David came up behind Randy

and slid one arm around his chest, just under the armpits. "Let go of the side for a second," David said.

Randy let go, but his hands remained clawed. David towed him a few feet, keeping Randy's head out of the water. "I'm going to pull you like this. You'll be backward. The only difference is you'll be holding your breath and you'll be under the water. Okay?"

"Okay." Randy grabbed for the rocks on the side again.

Neil realized he was now leaning forward with all his muscles tensed, as if trying to pump some kind of courage into Randy.

"Okay," David said. "Now all you have to do is relax, Randy. You're going to try and go limp and just concentrate on holding your breath. Okay? Because I'll tell you, frankly, my worst fear with you is that you're going to get scared and flail around or fight me and you're very strong. If you knock me out underwater . . . it won't be good."

"Yeah."

"I'm going to pull you down—a dive—and then we go straight and then we'll turn and go up toward the surface. When we break the surface, don't pull away from me because we won't be done. That water is rough and you need me to get to shore. Can you do all that?"

"Yeah."

"Okay," David said. "Come here." He put his arm around Randy again. Randy shook like a leaf as he let go of the rocks.

"I'm scared!" Terry whined.

"Shut up!" Neil shouted.

"Okay," David said patiently to Randy. "We're going to take three deep breaths together to stretch our lungs and then on the fourth, you hold your breath and off we go. Got it?"

"Yeah."

"You're gonna be all right, Rand," Neil said. "You couldn't be in better hands, there."

David glanced up at Neil, as if surprised, then focused on Randy again. "Comfortable?"

"Oh yeah," Randy said.

"Okay. Here we go. One, inhale and exhale."

Randy closed his eyes and breathed with David.

"Two, inhale really deep and exhale. Remember to hold it on four. Three, deep, deep and let it out. And now, four."

It was a horrible-looking maneuver, David pulling Randy under the water. It looked like murder. Neil felt a surge of panic, a sudden certainty that something would go wrong. He grabbed for a flashlight and beamed it down into the water. They were already gone.

Terry laid his hand on Neil's arm. "It's gonna be okay. Try to relax. There's nothing we can do."

"Yeah," Neil chanted almost to himself. "He's a fabulous swimmer. He's done things like this all his life. It's . . . it's fine."

"I'm scared," Terry said softly.

"You just told me not to be scared, you little asshole!" Neil shouted.

Terry flinched and put his arm up across his face.

Neil forced himself to calm down. "I'm crippled, Terry. Don't be scared of me. But Jesus, you can be exasperating sometimes."

"I know." He bowed his head, forelock dipping.

"Look, don't feel bad. We're all scared. You're just the one who says it."

"I know."

They sat quietly for a second, watching the water as if it might offer up clues. "David's really brave," Terry said.

"Yes, he is," Neil said.

"He's like . . . a hero," Terry said.

"Yes." Neil's throat closed unexpectedly. He turned his face away just in case.

"I'm sorry!" Terry said. "What did I say?"

Neil shook his head. "I don't know." He turned back to the water, struggling with himself. "I guess I wanted to be the hero."

After a second he felt a little pat on the arm. "But David *needed* it," Terry said.

Neil nodded. He couldn't speak for a second. Then he said, in a choked voice, "He's a good brother. A good person. He doesn't really know how good he is."

Terry nodded emphatically at the water. He hesitated and then said suddenly, "I love him."

The words echoed in the quiet, water-dripping chamber. Neil looked at Terry, trying to understand exactly what had been said and what it meant. After all, any friend might say that about any friend in a lifesaving situation. Terry was looking calmly at the water.

Neil tried to think of exactly the right thing to say. "I do, too," he said finally.

Terry smiled.

They didn't speak for several more seconds. "How long has it been?" Neil said.

Terry had pulled his knees up and rocked. "I don't know. That's what I was thinking. You don't think anything went wrong?"

"Well," Neil hated the fear he heard in his own voice. "In any situation something could go wrong. He did say the water up there was rough . . . and Randy's so impulsive. I guess that's what I'm worried about. Sometimes Randy can react like a spastic, you know? If he panicked, for instance—"

"He won't do that," Terry said. "This is life and death. I saw the way he killed that snake. He might be jumpy and all that, but when he has to concentrate, he concentrates. I'm more worried about David. Because he won't quit sometimes. If he's tired or he's losing, he just keeps going. I've seen it."

"Yeah, so have I," Neil said. "He can't stand to give up."

"We're making ourselves crazy," Terry said. "It just doesn't pay to think of this stuff."

Neil looked at Terry. "You know why I like you?" he said. "You really know how to take turns."

"What?"

"I just realized it. When anybody else gets scared, you reassure them. Then, when there's a lull and everybody else is feeling good, that's when you panic. It's so . . . polite of you!"

Terry laughed. "Yeah? Maybe that's true. Could I

have my turn now? Because I think it's been a long time . . ."

Neil looked at his watch. "Only three minutes. And we have to give them time to get Randy squared away on the bank. There's no telling how long it might take."

"Yeah. That's true." Terry giggled. "Okay, your turn. Get scared."

Neil was looking in the water. Far below, something gold was shining. "I don't have to!" he said, struggling to move closer to the water. "I think I see him!"

Terry grabbed the flashlight and they picked up David's hair, shiny as a carp. The surface of the water exploded with David. This time he wasn't even choking. "God! Wow! He did it! He's out! He—"

Neil reached for David, felt a sharp stab of pain and leaned back. "Get out of the water and rest! Then tell us."

David hauled himself out and plunked down in the dirt, oblivious to the mud he created. "He . . . Randy got right up on the bank and he was doing a victory dance . . . like . . . touchdown! Oh, you guys! This is so cool. This is the coolest thing. Who wants to be next?"

"You are as high as a kite on adrenaline, boy!" Neil told him. "Terry's next, but you rest until you're breathing normally, and drink some more water. This seems to dehydrate you."

David nodded, gasping.

"You don't have to be the last one," Terry said to Neil, "unless you want to."

221

"He has to," David said. "Neil has to be like the captain who goes down with his ship. Right?"

"Right." Neil was pleased he was still the captain. "What about Terry's breathing? I was wondering if he could actually take the oxygen underwater with him. Because I don't like the idea of an asthmatic holding his breath. . . . He could—"

"Yeah," David said. "Get in the water with your canister, Squirt, and see if it explodes in your face or anything. Too bad we didn't think of that for Randy. He was about blue."

Terry visibly relaxed at this idea. "Okay," he said and lowered himself carefully into the pool. Neil handed him his oxygen tank. "I hope there's enough," Terry said, fitting the strap over his shoulder. "There's an hour's worth in here but I haven't kept track of how much we've used." Terry put his face in the water like a scuba diver and took a few breaths of the oxygen. Then he bobbed up like a happy little bird. "It works!"

"Oh, this is almost too easy," David said, stretching his arms and legs. "I'm glad you're weighted down, Neil. I'm going to need a little challenge pretty soon. Are you ready to go, Terry?"

"Aren't you still out of breath?" Terry said hopefully.

"Nope. I'm ready to go." David got up and shivered like a dog to release the mud clinging to his back. He eased himself back in the water. "Okay?" he asked Terry.

"Well . . ."

Neil felt a squirm of panic. They were leaving him

alone! He might never see them again. He might die all alone in this fucking cave. "Hurry up," he said, almost involuntarily.

David threw his brother a brief, worried glance and then swam over to Terry. "Come on, Ter. It's now or never." He put his arm around Terry's chest. Terry began breathing oxygen.

"I'm still going to count to three, just so you'll know when we're diving," David said. "Okay?"

Terry nodded.

"One, two, three!" David said and pulled Terry under. Neil whimpered involuntarily. The agitated water slowly became still again. Stalactites dripped loudly. The stream laughed. Neil's heart beat fast. He was feeling several different things at once and he couldn't sort them all out.

There was a weird rustling behind him. Neil jumped so violently it made his broken leg throb. He looked up and saw a thin stream of bats flying into The Chamber, headed for their sleeping place in the ceiling. It was as if they knew the visitors were leaving and they could take their home back. Neil watched them slowly spiral toward the vaulted ceiling and then fold up like little drink umbrellas.

Neil thought his primary feeling was something like nostalgia or regret. Maybe he was going to miss this fucking death trap. He looked around at their scattered campsite, the backpacks and discarded clothes, the head of the shovel that was splinting his leg. He wanted to memorize things, burn the scene into his mind. He toyed with the limestone chunk in his hand, turned it over and looked at every bump and ridge in it. He really wanted to leave it there, not remember that horrible feeling of grasping on to rock and having it crumble into sand. But it was important. It was a feeling he knew he should remember. He rocked up on one hip and carefully slid the stone into his pocket.

A few more bats straggled in. They flew in a funny way, dipping every few feet and rising again. Neil looked at the calcite and remembered what it felt like under his feet. He remembered the beauty of The Chamber from the high ledges, the crystals that covered them with rainbows yesterday, the stars he'd watched through the hole in the ceiling.

Then Neil looked back at the pool. The water was agitating. He took a deep breath and let it out. David was coming. Everything was going to be all right.

The blond hair appeared again, rose, broke the surface. David thrashed a little this time, breathing hard. He was definitely tired. There was no grace in his strokes to the side of the pool. He was running on fumes.

Neil reached to help him. "You okay?"

"I . . ." (cough) "will be when we get you out. Let's go." David pulled Neil's arm.

"Uh-uh. I want to see you breathe like a person who isn't going to have a heart attack down there and let go of me and watch helplessly while my metal leg drags me to my death. Okay?"

"I'm fine!" David said. "Let's go!"

David was clearly coming unglued. This part of the mission unnerved him, for obvious reasons. Not a re-

assuring thing for Neil. He wanted a nice, calm res-
cuer with no emotional baggage.

"Chill," Neil said sternly. "I'm not kidding. The
only way you can screw up is to worry about screwing up. This is going to be fine. You did it twice before. Right?"

"Yeah," David nodded. "I know."

"Just give yourself three fucking minutes to get set.
Okay?"

"Yes."

Neil patted David's shoulder. "Good man. Terry
breathing okay?"

"Yes. Can I have some water?"

Neil filled Terry's empty canteen in the pool and
handed it over. David drank greedily, letting the ex-
cess run down his chest. "Why does being in the water make me so thirsty?" he said.

"Slow down," Neil said. "Don't choke."

"I know. Quit worrying about me." David put the
canteen down. "Okay, I feel pretty good. Just give me
one more minute to do some slow breathing."

"We have all day. Those guys out there aren't leaving without us."

"Have you got the car keys?" David said.

Neil patted his pocket. "Yeah. Boy, wouldn't it be
awful to leave them here? Then you'd have to make
another trip!"

David laughed. He seemed okay now. "Like fuck I
would." He picked up the canteen again.

"Hey," Neil said. "I'm really sorry I screwed up and
hurt myself and put all this on you."

David smiled a little. "No problem."

"But I feel like a jerk." Neil frowned at his leg. "I'm so useless."

"Neil, we survived. The important thing is we made it."

"Almost."

"We made it," David said firmly. "Are you ready?"

"Yeah, let's get this fucking nightmare over with." Neil dragged himself toward the water. He lowered his splinted leg in first. The downward pull was terrifying, as if he were wearing an anchor. David hovered, ready to grab if anything went wrong. But Neil got himself down in the water and waited for David to get into position behind him.

"Whatever you do," David said, "don't you dare accidentally kick me with that fucking piece of metal. Okay?"

Neil felt the water seeping into the gauze wrapped on his leg. His leg seemed to hurt more in the water, for some reason. "I promise," he said absently. He wondered what kind of medical treatment he was going to need when they got to a hospital and whether he was still going to be able to play basketball. Then he realized he was worrying about things that were trivial compared to a few hours ago, when he was trying to imagine what it was like to starve to death.

"Remember," David was lecturing. "You just let me do everything. You're more dangerous than Randy if you start trying to take over. Okay?"

"Okay," Neil said. "Get the show on the road."

"Okay. Count of four."

Something nervous jumped in Neil's stomach. "Okay."

"One . . . two . . ."

They breathed together. Neil had an urge to scream.

"Three . . . four!"

Neil pulled in a too-deep breath and a pain stabbed his chest. *Mistake.* Water rushed over his head. David was strong, pulled him swiftly, at a speed faster than Neil was used to swimming. Dark flowers of rock flashed past his eyes. The color was indescribable, something like turquoise, but also something like brown. Neil remembered his dream. *If I see a sign that says Cincinnati . . .*

Neil was looking backward, at his dead, stiff leg, which nauseated him. He twisted his head and saw David instead, muscles compressing and releasing efficiently, hair swirling like silk. Much better. And the water ahead was indeed shot through with sunlight. It looked bubbly and alive, full of movement and shadows. Neil's chest felt as if it were going to explode. He knew he needed to correct the overly deep breath he'd taken but he was afraid to exhale because once he started, his body might get giddy and try to do the whole breathing process, which would kill him. He blew out a few gentle bubbles. The pain subsided.

Then he felt a violent jolt to his whole body. His braced leg had struck and caught something, some jutting rock. David's grip was broken and for a second he just kept going on his forward momentum.

Neil looked down, alone and weighted, falling just as in his nightmare. Falling *slowly.* Just like Alice in the rabbit hole. Panic surged and he tried to swim, kicking his good leg and windmilling his arms.

He could hold even and stop falling, but not get anywhere. Despairingly, he realized how every second he was getting closer to the end of his lung capacity. He kicked more frantically, trying to look around and orient himself, trying to find that bright water again.

Then he saw David in the murk, doubling back like an eel. He swooped around, catching Neil under the arms and kicking so hard he kicked Neil in the spine. But that was okay; the point was to move forward. Neil tried to work with him, coordinating his own flailing to David's. David's chest was pressed against Neil's back and Neil could feel his brother's heartbeat, fast as a scared puppy's.

The water was brighter and bluer with every kick and flail. Neil's lungs ached. His leg throbbed. David turned them, and then they were swimming straight up.

Neil tipped his head back and saw the surface of the water, a dazzling blanket of light, lazily rippling above them. *Hold on, hold on, don't breathe!*

A surge. An explosion into oxygen. Light seared Neil's eyes as a cacophony of sound roared into his ears. He sucked in air, water, foam, anything, as his lungs went back to work. He vaguely heard Randy and Terry, screaming and cheering for them.

Little silver waves jumped across his vision. Every time he thought he saw something, he lost it again. David had shifted position and had Neil in a good lifeguard's grip now, pulling him through the rapids, into shallows.

Neil's good foot found a mushy purchase. His bad leg jarred painfully against the bank. People's hands were touching him, helping drag him up. His broken leg came out of the water last, dripping like the raised hull of a wrecked ship.

Then he was flat on his back on the riverbank, breathing with his whole body, just breathing and being alive, holding his eyes almost shut against the sunlight. He felt himself patted and touched and hugged.

Neil struggled to open his eyes against the glare and search for the most important thing in the mass of images and sounds. It was there. He reached for it. He pulled it into his arms. He called its name.

"David!"

Don't miss

The Spirit Window

by Joyce Sweeney

Fifteen-year-old Miranda doesn't know what to expect when she, her father, and her stepmother travel to Florida to visit her grandmother, who hasn't spoken to Miranda's father in ten years. First Miranda is shocked by energetic Grandma Lila. Soon something awakens in Miranda as she discovers the wildlife of the marsh Lila so fiercely protects.

Miranda captures nature's magic with her camera. She also captures Adam's heart. Part Cherokee, eighteen-year-old Adam cares for Lila's land and shares her passion for honoring wild creatures. Adam and Miranda share a physical attraction; besides that, Miranda admires Adam's belief in a sacred spirit world.

Miranda knows Lila's health is fragile but is caught off guard by her sudden death. Miranda's grief turns to confusion when Lila's will reveals that Adam will inherit her house, her land, and most of her money. Miranda's father, who had plans for the land, is furious and plots against Adam. Lila trusted her land to Adam believing he would uphold her values. Now Miranda wonders if Adam is all he seems to be.

For the first time, Miranda the perfect daughter must take a stand. The summer has changed her view of the world, from stark black and white to full color. But seeing more of the world is painful, too, as Miranda begins to turn the camera on her own life and past.

Fans of Joyce Sweeney's previous works will be intrigued by this story of explosive family tensions set against a backdrop of supernatural events.

0-385-32510-X